On the Run

Also by Angus Hall

Novels

Love in Smoky Regions (Constable, 1962)
Live Like a Hero (Hammond and Hammond, 1967)
Qualtrough (H. Jenkins, 1968)
A Long Way to Fall (W. H. Allen, 1971)

Diversions

The High-bouncing Lover (Hammond and Hammond, 1966)
The Come-uppance of Arthur Hearne (Hammond and Hammond, 1966)
The Late Boy Wonder (H. Jenkins, 1969)
The Gentle Sex (Sphere Books, 1972)

Occult

Devilday (Sphere Books, 1969)
To Play the Devil (Sphere Books, 1971)
Scars of Dracula (Sphere Books, 1971)

On the Run

by

ANGUS HALL

HARRAP LONDON

First published in Great Britain 1974
by George G. Harrap & Co. Ltd
182-184 High Holborn, London WC1V 7AX

ISBN 0 245 52142 9

Printed and bound in Great Britain by
REDWOOD BURN LIMITED
Trowbridge & Esher

For Andrew – when he is old enough to recognize himself in his double role.

Every day there's this sudden coldness in my hands and feet. I start to tremble and my teeth chatter. It's when I pick up a newspaper or turn on the TV or radio . . . What I'm expecting and dreading, what makes me so trembling and sick in the stomach, is to hear that the hunt is over.

Mrs Charmian Biggs
(wife of Ronald Biggs, the
Great Train Robber, in an article
in the *Sunday Mirror*, 1969)

GLOSSARY

Banged-up: locked in cell for night.
Baas: boss.
Bird: prison sentence.
Blag merchant: payroll bandit.
Boomeranging: returning to prison.
Carpet: three months' sentence.
Charlie Chaplin: prison chaplain.
Charver: sexual intercourse.
Claret: blood.
Earnings: proceeds from robbery or crime.
Filth: The C.I.D.
Firm: criminal gang.
Form: previous convictions.
Gas-meter bandits: small-time crooks.
Goby: criminal go-between.
Grass: to inform.
Handful: five-year sentence.
Horse: heroin.
Jelly baby: gelignite expert.
Jumbo: raw and stupid police constable.
Kapenaar: someone born in Cape Town.
Linen: newspapers.
Million: a certainty.
Mug-shots: prison photographs.
Mystery: a girl about to be picked up.
Nineteen canteen: a long time ago.
Peter: cell.
Proovy: approved school.
Pull a stroke: successfully commit a crime.
Rabbiting: gossiping.
Rep: crook or convict with status.
Richard: a girl.
Screw: prison officer or guard.
Skelm: a rogue.

Slaughter: safe place for keeping and distributing proceeds from a crime.
Smother-up: wear a mask, or stocking during the execution of a crime.
Smudge merchant: street photographer.
Sobs: pound notes.
SP: starting price or information.
Stiff: illicit mail or letter, smuggled into or out of prison.
Stir: prison.
Stoep: verandah.
Stretch: prison sentence (usually of one year).
Suss: to suspect.
Tomfoolery: jewels, diamonds.
Topped: hanged.
Threed-up: put three-in-a-cell.
Tronk: police station.
Twoer: two hundred pounds.
Vet: prison doctor.

PHASE ONE

CHAPTER ONE

She was already waiting when he entered the visiting-room, sitting in a low wooden-armed chair, her knees pressed close together, her hands clasping them as if doing some rudimentary yoga exercise. Her head was turned away from him, looking out at the grey tarmac of marshland that stretched to the North Sea – a dark line edging the grey like an in-mourning border on a piece of grubby notepaper. Immediately he noticed things about her; perhaps new things, or old things he'd forgotten about since he'd last seen her. Her hair, very black and curly, had been chopped short so that the curls sprang up like sawdust shavings, or the coils of wire you see protruding from old and broken mechanisms. She was thinner, had lost weight in a way that made her bony-looking and threatfully neurotic. She was a distortion, a mirror-image of the girl he'd known and pleasured and enjoyed. But it was the way she crouched there, hunched and defensive, that made him think of her as caged.

A prison officer moved to the side of her – returned to his metal desk and clipboard by the door – causing her to swing round as though she had committed some unknown, accidental offence. Blake saw her eyes, the colour of charcoal, the turned-up spout of her nose, her mouth that was too long and prominent for her V-shaped face. Then he noticed the tiny, hair-like lines over her upper lip; worry lines that resembled the beginnings of a narrow moustache. She needed love and loving to make her flourish again, to be a beautiful instead of a withered twenty-seven. He wondered if he was still capable of supplying that.

'Hello . . . Philip.'

The man smiled, took the chair beside her, unfastened her hands from her knees and wrapped them in his own chunky red fingers. Despite the gasfire behind them spitting sullen blue-and-yellow flames, her flesh was cold, a frozen bandage on matchwood bones. The man looked around at the rest of the reunited husbands and wives in the partitioned-off room. Most of them had their children with them. All of them talking, moving, scuffling, crying; anxious to be there, impatient to be gone. All except his own two – Alastair and Ian – who were where?, and with whom?

He tightened his grasp on her; she winced and tried to pull her hands away, to unscrew them at the wrist, leaving them behind her like spares.

'Why didn't you bring the boys, Karen?' he asked thickly.

'Here? To this place? To see their father in prison?'

'Where do they think I am. On a space mission?'

'I told you in my letters—'

'All nine of them.'

' . . . they think you're in South Africa, working.'

'With my dear father-in-law.'

'With daddy.'

He sighed, relaxed his hold, watched her retrieve her hands, examine them as if they'd just come back from a repair shop. Now that his own hands were free he found they wanted to crawl away from him to lead their own separate life – two boiled lobsters grabbing at each other, teasing and nipping with fat vermilion feelers. They wrestled for a while; then, honours even, parted and moved sideways across his thighs, disappeared beneath his legs so that he was half sitting on them and they were half supporting him. He had been told he had farmer's hands; although no farmer would have traded his for them . . .

'I came because I had to talk to you. There are things you can't *say* properly in a letter.'

'Not even in a "Dear John"?'

'I'm not leaving you, Philip. If that's what you're hoping for.'

He didn't answer, waited for her to continue. Nine months without seeing her, without hearing her, and she not only looked but sounded different. Being married to him for six years, and living first of all on the farm and then in a dormitory suburb of London, had made him think of her as English. A nicely spoken young English-woman with a correct English accent. Now he realized how much of an outsider she really was. An actress who'd been playing a part, and, now that the run was over, had reverted to her normal, unanglicized self. Her voice again had that peculiar, boxed-in, Hebrewish quality that many white South Africans possess. He'd have to get used to her staccato way of speaking again. And a whole lot else besides.

'Where would I go to if I did?'

He gave a verbal shrug.

'Home to Cape Town.'

'And hear those four little words I hate most in the world.'

'"I told you so".'

'Daily. From everyone. Everywhere.'

'So what's the alternative?'

'We stick together. You can always get another job.'

'Failed embezzler, 49, seeks position in office where the tills don't have mousetraps.'

She pointedly didn't laugh.

'It's not impossible. You're not a criminal. You're only . . .'

'Unfortunate. I broke the eleventh commandment. Thou Shalt Not Be Found Out.'

'Surely they must teach you *some*thing in here. Train you to fend for yourself when you get out.'

He felt his hands protest at this; emerge from hiding to give evidence if needed.

'I've learned a really useful trade so far. Well-paid, too. Brings in all of fifty pence a week.'

Her face betrayed two things: distaste at the word 'trade'; interest in the fact that he'd not been malingering.

'It's called "dismants", and requires the maximum of skill and brainpower.'

'Dismants?'

'Dismantling old bits of telephone cable and electrical equipment.'

'But Philip – what for?'

'To extract the various metals from them. The Home Office considers it extremely valuable and worthwhile. A true vocation.'

'Like sewing mailbags.'

'Don't knock it. I've done that as well.'

His hands took their cue and climbed into the witness-box before her. She looked at the recently-healed cuts, where the skin had been rubbed away and had peeled from the sides and tips of the fingers. Purplish they were now, like the face of a drunk.

'Just try it sometime,' he said. 'Eight waxed stitches to the inch, and all done by hand. In here we're still waiting for the Industrial Revolution to start.'

'I'm sorry, Phil. I didn't know.'

'You're in the majority.'

Silence came between them cold as the late March snow that fluttered moth-like at the windows, hundreds of soft white wings beating to get in. Beyond that, undeterred by the weather, he could see the lorries that came daily from Norwich and Great Yarmouth, stacked with all manner of junk and rubble, which, after lowering their tails like insects defecating, they deposited on the marshes.

The woman, Karen, gave a small, dismissive cough, consulted her heart-shaped wristwatch with the emerald and ruby numerals.

'There's another ten minutes yet before they blow the whistle,' the man said.

'I'd better go now. It's taken me half the day to get here. If I miss my connection I'll probably have to sleep on the beach. As I understand some of the wives do.'

'That's what they say about prison; it's almost a holiday.'

'Besides,' she went on, 'I left the boys with Mrs Willard across the way. *She* has a social life to lead in the evenings, even if some of us don't. You weren't the only person to be sentenced, you know. The boys and I were too.'

He fumbled for something – anything – to say.

'It's nice of Mrs Willard to take them.'

'She's been very helpful and . . . loyal.'

'The only one I suppose.'

'The *main* one.'

'It's reassuring to know how good neighbourly our good neighbours are. The "Samaritans of Carlton Close".'

'Yes. They've been awfully kind, considering.' She paused. 'To me.'

'My reception being yet to come.'

She rose the instant before he did, stood arched and defiant, the top of her head level with his shoulders. Now that she'd learned what his letters hadn't definitely told her – he *was* returning to her after his release; he didn't intend to continue his inglorious career of crime – her womanhood and sexuality flowed pinkly into her. As though too shy to let him see this, she made a ceremony of putting on her fur-lined suede gloves.

'And when can we expect you home?'

'I'll have done my bird in another three months.'

'You'll have . . .?'

From their correspondence she knew what he meant, but it made her feel superior, less contaminated to pretend ignorance.

'I shall be out after serving a final carpet.'

'And then what?'

'I promise you one thing, Karen. I'll never lean on you for support again.'

'You have plans?'

'Moneymaking ones.'

'As long as they're legal.'

'They're better than legal. They'll work.'

'Good. Then we'll be waiting for you.'

Before he could ask her about the boys, she had started towards the door, picking her way through the kids squatting cross-legged on the floor like junior mystics, their Hong Kong-manufactured cars overturned and abandoned; past the rubber overshoes of the wives and mothers; the brownpaper carrier-bags beside them, bulging with sliced bread and fishfingers bought in the depressed village which gave Manston its name; around the apologetic feet of the cons themselves, tucked quickly beneath them as her knee-length leather boots (dark and shiny as seals) splashed and dived among them. The man followed her mutely, conscious of the effect she was making, like a film-star returning to the slums of her birth on an obligatory publicity tour.

As she reached the door the screw Jack-in-the-boxed to his feet, alert and respectful, and opened it for her. She thanked him with a slight incline of her head, then looked at her husband as though he'd applied for a post with her but had been rejected due to inferior references.

'Are we allowed to embrace?' she asked formally.

He nodded. 'Providing you don't transfer any drugs into my mouth.'

He bent down, found her lips, felt them open under his like those of a hungry young bird. During his entire stretch he hadn't as much as kissed the back of his own hand. ('That's what you're married to from now on,' one of the cons had told him in his first week inside. 'Your right hand is your wife, mate.') Kissing her was like sampling a new and exotic food; rich, stimulating, rare. Then, by way of a bonbon, she flicked her tongue into his mouth – a quick exploration and out again, but enough to send his heart and stomach catherine-wheeling.

She left without a 'Darling' or farewell, and he watched her clip down the green linoleum corridor, her heels tapping out a message of confidence and hope, the fur trimming on the bottom of her Cossack coat bobbing like the tail of a thoroughbred horse.

The screw closed the door with his foot, winked at him and smirked.

'That's some Richard you got yourself there, Blake.'

'Thanks,' the man said. 'She *is* an attractive girl.'

For a millionaire's daughter, he added silently.

CHAPTER TWO

She left the prison hurriedly as if aware that comments were being made about her figure, her hair, her style, her clothes. Shrinking into herself, she avoided the other visitors, their faces more ashamed and lost than those of the prisoners themselves. She wished her suede coat was not so long, so furry, so expensive. She flinched at the noise it made, like fingers rubbing on wet glass, as it slapped against her luminous leather boots.

Her walk through the prison yard, and out through the gate, was stiff and awkward. She kept her head down and twice stumbled as she stared at, but failed to see, the stones and ridges in the ground. She could have been walking on stilts, or learning to do so.

The man in the car watched her approaching and started the engine. He leant across the passenger seat, opened the door, and settled back, his thumbs tapping industriously on the steering-wheel. The woman glanced up, saw the Jaguar crouching before a background of snow, marshland, more snow falling. She remembered the headscarf in her pocket, and put it on as she covered the last few yards between her and her escort.

She ducked her head, slid into the car, banged the door behind her. The man said nothing. He eased the Jaguar forward, semi-circled away from the prison and its cobbled forecourt. The car cut black trace-lines on the hill that curved down to the village. For a while the couple didn't talk but listened to the silence of the snow, the swish of tyres, the asthmatic breathing of the windscreen-wipers.

Then, as the car turned onto the highway to Norwich and London, Karen looked over at the man. Saw the hearing-aid tucked like a pink plastic claw behind his left ear. He had been waiting for her to do so, and spoke impersonally, not taking his eyes from the road.

'Well, how did it go?'

Although it wasn't necessary, she raised her voice.

'It could have been worse.'

'But it could have been better.'

'I don't know.' She paused and pulled at her headscarf. 'He's not at all as I expected.'

'The bitter, cynical con.'

'Oh, he's that all right. But he's not defeated. He hasn't given up.'

'Given up what? Crime?'

'He talks as if he has. He's quite positive and optimistic.'

'Aren't they always – until the next time?'

Her lips lengthened.

'He's not an old lag, you know. A receptivist or whatever they're called.'

'Recidivist.'

'He made a stupid and untypical mistake. He's paying for it now, and he won't be as idiotic again.'

'I'm glad you think so, Karen.'

'Don't you?'

The man with the hearing-aid shifted in the bucket seat.

'There's something about him I don't trust. And never have done.'

'But you've never even met him!'

'I don't have to. I've studied his Army career, his civilian career, everything about him. I've added all I've learned together. Checked and rechecked the result.'

'And?'

'It adds up right. Which is precisely what's wrong with it!'

'I'm sorry, I don't—'

'It's all too pat, too self-explanatory, too natural. The progress of his crime is so logical it doesn't ring true. There should have been a flaw somewhere — a kink, a tangent. But he went as straight as an arrow in the wrong direction.'

'You think there should have been—'

'A slight pull to the left or right. A deviation.'

'Perhaps there was and you didn't spot it.'

'I'm still looking!'

'You've been awfully good. All the trouble you've gone to. Seeing I was all right at home and driving me out here. You didn't have to do it.'

'I had to be in London, though. And life isn't all business.'

'There should also be pleasure.'

'To me this is pleasure. I'm peculiar that way!'

The man with the hearing aid laughed – joylessly and without humour. Karen turned her head from him, also gazed rigidly at the road.

'I'll have to go back to him. For the time being at least.'

'For the boys' sake?'

'Partly. But also for his. He needs me now just as I needed him once. I'm not prepared to fail him.'

'Or leave him?'

'Not yet. Perhaps not ever. I'm sorry, but that's the way it is. I don't expect you to understand—'

'But I do,' the man interrupted. 'I understand perfectly. I just don't appreciate it.'

'I'd like to tell you more about Philip. More than you've learned from your investigations and reports. The little private things that make a man of him and not just a case-history. Like the way he always—'

Unnoticed by her, the man with the hearing-aid put his hand to his ear, turned the instrument off. He wasn't interested in Blake the man, the husband, the father. He was obsessed with Blake the crook. Obsessed with watching him, tracking him, anticipating him. Obsessed with putting him back inside — or making a fugitive of him.

CHAPTER THREE

It wasn't until he was back in the dismantling shop – an echoing, hangar-like building tacked onto the side of the main block – that Blake realized he hadn't told Karen the truth. About his going straight.

He knew this as he passed between the two discipline officers, erect on their tall wooden thrones, supervising the endless and futile labour, and rejoined the team he worked with. At once the human sounds of the visiting-room were banished and replaced by the non-stop cacophony of splintering wood, breaking metal, the pop music that screeched from grey loudspeakers stuck like disembodied mouths on the girders above their heads.

None of the others – the two middle-aged cons in for armed robbery; the two younger ones, both ex-Borstal boys, who'd been done for trafficking in drugs – commented on his return. They had spent the morning and early afternoon uncoiling yards of copper wire from disused telephone equipment. As a 'red band', or trusted prisoner, he was supposed to see that the others worked at the right prison pace. Not too fast so that a day's work was done in a day and not a week; not so slow that someone fell asleep across his bench, as sometimes happened.

They nodded to each other and he grasped a stout length of twisted wire which felt like thread in his hands. There was almost an hour to go before they were herded into the mess, were fed and watered, and banged-up for the night. Seeing Karen again (he didn't blame her for not coming before; hospitals and all places of impersonal authority made her nervous) had taken him out of Manston, away from Norfolk, back to the London of the mid-sixties when he had turned bolshy and quit the department. It was an embarrassing experience admitting to people that he worked for Defence Intelligence, sixth section, (DI6 to the Press and public), and that his job was mainly concerned with counter-espionage, stopping foreign agents and traitors from transmitting national secrets abroad.

'I work for the War Office, actually,' he used to say to their questions. 'Just another desk-bound civil servant, I'm afraid.'

'Come off it, old boy. That's not what our taxes are being spent on. Dirty weekends in Istanbul and Beirut more like it.'

'No. Really. I go to a little office in Whitehall each morning, spend most of the day on the 'phone or dictating memos, and come peacefully home to my bed-sitter at night.'

He'd told Karen that on the evening he'd first met her at one of the occasional perks he got, a cocktail party at South Africa House in honour of some politician fresh in from Union Building, Pretoria. She, too, had regarded him with her head on one side and her eyes knowing.

'It's quite true,' he stressed. 'I've been there ever since I left the Army. Pensioned-off and too old at thirty-five.'

She sipped her Coca-Cola and politely disbelieved him.

'You were in the war, then? And I don't mean the cold one.'

'A sergeant in the commandos. Promoted to captain on the field of battle at Anzio, January '44. I was one of the youngest officers in our mob and one of the luckiest.'

'How?'

'I didn't get killed on the beach head. Many of us did.'

'You must have been very brave.'

'Or very lucky. We spent most of our time waiting under fire. For the rains to stop. For the allies to join us. Four months of that and then we got through the German lines, and pushed on to Rome.'

'Then you were a hero.'

'And/or psychopath.'

This time she looked genuinely puzzled.

'I don't understand your meaning.'

'Only that most of the so-called heroes I knew, and that included a posthumous VC, were a combination of murderer, crook and thug. In peacetime they'd have been behind bars. During the war the only bars they saw were the ones added to their medals.'

'You sound very cynical. Is that why you're a spy now?'

'Government clerical officer. Yes, I expect so. I've always lived off this country, and now I'd like to do so literally.'

'How do you mean?'

'Start a farm. A tomato farm. Somewhere down in Sussex or Kent.'

'Where the sun shines.'

'That doesn't matter. Most tomatoes are grown under glass nowadays. You raise them from seed early in the year. Even the late fruit can be ripened in the dark.'

'Quite the expert.'

'Lots of people are in England.'

'Don't be modest. I've always *liked* tomatoes.'

'So have I. You know what they used to be called?'

She shook her head, and her hair — it was longer then and silkier – fell like a velvet curtain across her face.

'Can't imagine.'

'Love apples.'

'But that's charming!'

'I'd like to give you some sometime; home-grown, of course.'

'Naturally.'

'In fact, I'll go one better than that. I'll invite you down to my farm to choose your own. Cultivated personally with my own outsize hands.'

'And the hands of your wife.'

'Yes, I'd need a wife to help me.'

'Is the position open to applicants?'

'I hadn't seriously thought about it.'

'Then I should do so. Now.'

Four weeks after that he handed in his resignation to the War Office, and married Karen Petersen, 21, only daughter of Theo Petersen, chairman and managing director of White Star Insurance, Heerengracht, Cape Town. They got a mortgage on Love Apple Farm (as they renamed it), near Hythe, and Karen found herself cut off with the traditional shilling, or, in her case, South African rand. There were things about herself she hadn't told him – and didn't confess – until their cut-price, economy honeymoon.

'It's not so much that Daddy is anti-British,' she said. 'Although he is, of course, and always supported General Hertzog. It's just that, well, I was supposed to marry someone else this month. Back home in St George's Cathedral.'

'Someone else?' In bed this, after lovemaking.

'Mark Kretzmer. He's one of Daddy's brightest young men. Set to take over the company in due course.'

'And you were the first rung on his climb to the top.'

'Which is why I came to England for a month. To think things over and let Mark know definitely one way or the other.'

'And have you?'

'I sent him a cable the day after I met you.'

'But you might never have seen me again. I could have disappeared, or stood you up on our first date.'

She smiled teasingly.

'My answer to that would have been lethal and inescapable.'

'Why, what would you have done?'

'Put DI6 on your trail!'

He knew then why her father hadn't been asked to their wedding (not in any cathedral, but a registry office in Fulham, where he lived); why Petersen had only been told about it after the event; why there'd been a private detective snooping around, disinterring his more or less average private life, background and past; why, ever since then, Karen had not been home; and why, on his annual visits of inspection to his London office, Petersen entertained Karen and the children in his penthouse suite at the Connaught, without his son-in-law being present.

He had never seen the man, yet had taken precious, personal things from him: daughter, authority, pride. And now that he was soon to leave Manston – he was going to take something which would hurt and distress Petersen even more. He was going to relieve him and his company of three million pounds.

He must have gone into a trance just thinking about it. The first he knew about being injured was when one of the older cons, a squint-eyed Scotsman called Rob, shouted a warning that was muted by the clanking of metal and guitar.

'Look out, mon. It's amuck!'

He glanced down and saw that the tautly held copper wire had snapped at the end where it was embedded in a piece of equipment – all angles and rusted nodules – that resembled an improvised sculpture. With the four others behind him straining like a tug-of-war team, it tore jaggedly through his hands, an instrument of edges, fibres and knots. Blood appeared between his fingers like the filling in a sandwich cake. He dropped the wire to the ground, where it formed a gingery figure-of-eight. Rob came closer and examined his hands as if they were specimens in a bottle.

'You'd better go sick with those, mon.'

Usually he avoided the prison doctor as much as he did the resident Charlie Chaplin – a dough-faced, slack-jawed clergyman who answered all problems with the insight and originality of an advice-to-the-lovelorn columnist. Today, however, he felt the need to get away from his cell and its two other occupants. Intimate strangers who seldom gave him scope to think. The discipline officer he showed his hands to agreed with Rob.

'Don't mess up my shop with your claret,' he snapped. 'Take your bleedin' paws to the vet.'

CHAPTER FOUR

The vet told him his hands were hurt more badly than he'd thought. He spent three days in the hospital; first of all in bed, and then slouching around the ward with his fingers wrapped-up like slices of raw meat. This period of time out, the first he'd had since entering Manston, gave him a chance to put his plans about Karen's father and the dividend he was going to collect into perspective. But it wasn't until he was discharged, and told to report for light duties, that he was able to mention them, discuss them with somebody else.

It was 11.30, lunchtime, as he left the hospital and crossed the walled-in exercise yard between it and 'B' Wing, where he was housed. He bypassed the cons who were walking in supervised groups of two and three – failures not only in life but in crime as well. He tried not to look in their faces; avoiding the defeat and weakness etched there like the maps of lost battles. At six feet one, and with his tawny hair sprouting like a coxcomb, he felt twice the drab, stunted creatures who said little that wasn't a whine of protest about the unfairness of their sentence, the iniquity of the police, the hopelessness of being inside. His training and discipline in the department and, before that, the Army and boarding school, had inured him to prison conditions.

He believed in rules, order, system. While not what he'd call a deep-thinking man, he felt there was an underlying pattern to the universe, one that should be reflected in the way people arranged and governed their lives. He enjoyed living by the rule book, being told what to do providing it was positive and made practical sense.

He stopped at the cusped, iron-studded door leading to the recreation room in which he and two hundred others ate their diet of bread, gruel, dry vegetables and chalky potatoes. Despite the wind that came buffeting across the yard, he caught a last sour whiff of the prisoners as he opened the door and moved inside.

'B' Wing was like the three other variously-sized blocks that made up Manston. It was oblong-shaped with turrets at each corner which were used as offices and storerooms, and had three rows of cells laid one on top of each other like seams in a coal mine. The recreation room was a space in the well of the building, filled with long trestle tables and benches without backs. Usually he ate at table three – together with a rapist, a boomeranging gas-meter bandit, a jelly baby, a murderer, and a couple of villains who had real rep. But today he couldn't face their piggish manners and looks. He approached the duty officer with the hole the size of a split pea in his forehead, and displayed his still-bandaged hands.

'What's the matter then Blake?' the officer asked indifferently. 'Been feastin' on your fingernails?'

'Something like that, sir. I'm not hungry. I thought I'd go to the library and read.'

'At this hour? The library's shut and you know it.'

'Bartholomew will let me in.'

'Like that is it? Librarian's bum-boy!'

Blake clamped his teeth together and grinned.

'Thought I'd catch up on my reading, sir. The only linen the vet had was a year-old copy of *War Cry*.'

The officer shrugged his assent and Blake walked away with anger tightening his chest. To reach his destination, he had to go between the tables, past the serving-hatch, into the high connecting corridor that led like the spoke of a wheel to the nucleus of chapel, prison shop, reading room and library.

As the screw had warned, the library was officially closed but he could see Bart, Donald Bartholomew, through the twin postage stamps of glass that served as windows. He was sitting behind his counter, a fat, bald-headed, pumpkin of a man with eyes like a teddy-bear's, doing the crossword puzzle in one of the tabloid dailies. He kneed open the swing-doors and Bart looked up blinking.

'Welcome to Tiny Tots' Corner,' he said, dropping the paper onto his lap.

Blake nodded behind him to the half-a-dozen shelves of thrillers, westerns and defaced biographies that were lent, two a week, to the prisoners.

'I thought this was the seat of all learning.'

'More like the anus.'

'Better than slaving in a building gang.'

'With my heart? I shouldn't even be stamping the issue cards!'

'The rich, quiet life; that's what we're all after.'

He waited while Bart fiddled in the pocket of his grey prison shirt, with the blue band on the sleeve indicating he was a leader, and free to move without escort. Bart produced what looked like two lengths of straw and offered one to him.

'Here, have a burn.'

'No, thanks.'

'Cancer threat scare you?'

'Cigarettes are like most vices – I can take but not always leave them.'

'Wise man.'

Bart struck a match, lit up, swallowed the smoke greedily, as if it was oxygen.

'So what else is new?' Blake asked casually.

'Zero. And with you?'

Blake hesitated, uncertain whether to forget all about crime, wild justice and riches. Then he leaned over the librarian, saw the sweat that lay like cold sores on his lips.

'Name me the number one topic of conversation in here.'

'What is this – *Twenty Questions*?'

'For a world record prize.'

Bart frowned and shuffled the possibilities in his mind.

'Having it away?' he hazarded.

'More popular even than escaping. Come on, man, you know the answer better than I do.'

'The Big Job?'

'Right second go. The Big Job.'

'Last time I was in the Scrubs they were all rabbiting about that. A mysterious Mr X in the background, and a haul of two million plus.'

'And what was done about it?'

'Plenty. It was more than only gossip. On 8th August 1963, it came as true as an honest man's confession.'

'Why, what happened then?'

'Only the Great Train Robbery.'

That was it; the moment when Blake's plan gave birth or miscarried.

He lowered his voice and spoke each word separately, as though dictating a telegram.

'I have something better, and bigger, than that.'

Bart took up his pen and nonchalantly completed 4-across.

'Go ahead,' he encouraged. 'Clue me in.'

CHAPTER FIVE

From their meetings and conversations comparing notes Blake knew more about Bart and his background than about any of the other cons, including the two with whom he shared his cell. Bart was what used to be called 'an educated man'. He had attended a public school which had been founded by monks in the sixteenth century, and then spent a couple of terms at Cambridge before being rusticated and finally sent down. Originally his occupation had been that of accountant to a chain of gambling and drinking clubs in the West End. His one-way passion for blackjack and dice had made him run to seed and race into debt. Later he looked after the books for one of the Soho protection gangs, and then set up on his own as a kind of backroom brain organizing several coups which, for a time at least, had baffled and embarrassed the police.

He rarely played visible roles in these jobs, leaving the physical work to the 'firms' who engaged him.

'I'm a consultant,' he'd informed Blake during the first of their chats. 'A consultant in crime. They name it, I plan it. The only connection I have with the villains is a financial one. Once they've picked my brains and paid me, I sever the cord.'

This was the kind of detached expertise Blake needed if he was to succeed where no-one else had so far tried. He liked the way Bart listened to him – head bent over his puzzle, ballpoint active – taking in everything he said; sorting, filing, cross-referencing for future use.

'You see this,' he was fond of saying, tapping the wrinkled yellow vault of his head. 'What do you think is in there? Grey matter? The usual mass of nervous tissue, ventricles and lobes? Then you're wrong. There's a computer boxed in there – one that never fuses or errs!'

Blake believed and trusted in him because he had to. There was no-one else he could confer with. No-one else who would listen to his scheme without interruption or jibe. He told him about the farm first of all; how Karen and he had worked it for a year and how they had failed. She just wasn't cut out for farming; her instincts and reflexes were wrong. Unlike him, she couldn't bend with the seasons, do things not because she wanted to, but because it was the necessary time of year.

Even so, they still might have swung it if it hadn't been for Alastair who chose that time to be conceived and carried. Once she was pregnant, her upbringing and expectations asserted themselves. He was no longer married to Karen Petersen, a girl he had seduced (or been seduced by) after a party. He was hitched to a rich man's daughter who was not prepared to take her swollen belly to the outside lavatory, or draw water from a pump, or cook breakfast in an unheated stone kitchen, or iron the damp out of the sheets, or deal with any of the hundred other chores and inconveniences that go with a thatched and ill-ventilated farmhouse.

'It's no use, I tell you,' she shouted in the middle of one of their rows. 'I'm a city girl. I like smog, and asphalt, and noise. This is like living in the veld. Five miles to the nearest town, and another million from civilization!'

'I'm sorry, Kar. What do you want me to do about it?'

'Sell up before either I go mad or you go bankrupt.'

'But we're just starting to show a profit. A return on our money.'

'Profit!' Her voice shrilled and eyes dilated. 'You call twelve pounds a week profit!'

'Some people would.'

'Some people would eat pigwash. Not me!'

'Who will I sell the place to?'

'What do I care. Someone sold it to you, didn't they? There's one born every minute.'

It was getting dark at the time, the first skirmish with winter, and he lit the ornate Victorian oil-lamp with the patterned glass funnel and black ivory stand.

'Even if I do that what happens then? I can hardly go back to the department. When I left they regarded me almost as a security risk.'

'If it's a choice between my baby and the bread line, I'll get daddy to fix you up with something.'

'In insurance, I suppose?'

'That's right. In bloody insurance!'

It was then, however belatedly, that he discovered something very basic about himself. He could give orders to men, arrange their lives and careers so that they would die for Queen, honour and country if told to. Yet he could not handle a girl young enough to be his daughter, who had made a god of him only a few months before. At Karen's insistence, he transferred the deeds in the farm to an elderly couple who had not saved enough to retire to sunny Majorca. The money obtained installed them in a new and more suitable house, and he faced the future with guarded optimism.

All this happened during one month. By November he had been taken on as assistant surveyor in the fire department of White Star Insurance Co. Ltd, in their City office; an antiseptic steel-and-glass lung in Paul's Pier, leading down to the Thames. He was an echelon higher – and several years older – than the junior clerks who did the routine work of collecting and distributing the mail, answering the 'phone, filing and keeping the records. He worked at a green tubular desk in a fifth-storey room lit by strips of fluorescent, with a round electric clock above his head, and the continual road-drill noise of typewriters, cheque-writing and adding machines. He earned just over £750 a year, and attended night school classes in economics and commerce so that he might eventually be admitted to the Chartered Insurance Institute when he would receive around twenty pounds for a five-day week, with two weeks' paid holiday a year.

'I know it's hard for you, Phil, with your experience and at your age,' admitted Karen. 'But what's the alternative?'

For a long time he wondered about that himself. Although Petersen had pulled all the required strings, no-one in the building knew of their relationship. That was one of the conditions Petersen insisted upon when replying to Karen's hard-luck letter.

'It's just that he's too proud and independent to admit that his son-in-law's a—' She groped for the euphemism.

'A flop.'

'A man who's embarking on a new career, and has yet to make a success of it. It takes time, darling, and courage.'

'Courage I have the medals to prove. It's time I'm running out of.'

But time continued, and he thought about the alternative, and one day it walked into his office, came up to his desk, and blatantly solicited him. He had learned a lot during his unwanted career in insurance; particularly that the business was like a gambling game in which the clients (or suckers) made the bets; the agent (or croupier) spun the wheel; and the company (or bank) usually won. As with all forms of gambling it attracted crooks in the manner of a casino or racecourse. And the punter who came to see him that glad summer morning was about as straight as the Great Wall of China.

He had the mannerisms and appearance of a petty official, the sort who uses authority as a club. Hands washing one another with invisible soap; leaky opaque eyes and hair freckling the collar of his ready-made serge suit; a white crust giving substance to his bacon-rind lips. About Blake's age, but looking older, thinner, more worn.

It took only five minutes of innuendo and half-voiced suggestions for Blake to realize that the client – who owned a one-man joke and novelty shop near Tower Bridge – was seeking a fiddle, a wangle, a spot of easy larceny. A year earlier Blake would have spat the bait into the man's face. But he had already made up his mind to use White Star to his own gain even if it meant going to prison for it. And once in gaol where better, he reasoned, to find and form a gang for the major coup to come? The seedy, insinuating client and he were made for each other. With the joke shop due to be demolished in 1973 and replaced by high-rise apartments, the customer hinted that it would be 'convenient' to him if his fire policy could be 'amended' to cover the remaining period of his lease.

'I've got my compensation money coming to me,' he said slyly. 'But I thought a little insurance payout would be nice in the event of an . . . unfortunate fire.'

Nice, and stupid, and bound to be pounced on by the claims' manager, thought Blake. Nearly fifty percent of all the claims put in were phony. They were spotted and the matter usually ended there, without prosecution. But if he – to use the legal term – aided and abetted the crime, then he would be inside quicker than it took to add a loop to the top of a '6' on all three copies of the client's policy extending coverage by two months.

It was a stupid, clumsy deception and one that deserved to be unmasked. It soon was – the moment the manager returned from a refresher course to find a fire claim on a building no company would have risked a halfpenny on. The manager called Blake idiotic and disloyal, and the judge at his trial called him something worse.

'It is sad to find a former Army officer and civil servant before me in this court,' he said fussily. 'But to appear on a charge of champerty is a tragedy and a disgrace. To have deliberately connived with a client to swindle his employers and then share in the illgotten gains, is something quite beyond my comprehension.'

Blake imagined that it was. But he stood upright and soldierly as he received the sentence he wanted. Not so long that he would go stir-crazy. Not so short that he would be unable to make the contacts he needed. Eighteen months with a third remitted for possible co-operation and good conduct.

He thanked the judge when it was over. Bowed to him and was taken down to the cells with his hand over his mouth. Striving valiantly not to laugh.

* * *

'Most instructive,' said Bart, as Blake's account and his puzzle dead-heated to an end. 'Pity they don't make those "Crime Doesn't Pay" films any more. Your script would be a natural. Only I don't see what it has to do with a Big Job. Unless you propose insuring this place and burning it to the ground.'

'Give me a chance,' Blake protested. 'That was just the prologue. I haven't got to the part about the diamonds yet.'

'Diamonds?' He repeated the word as if it was new to him, and he was sounding it out.

'Three million pounds'-worth of them. Insured for that by White Star in South Africa, and flown each year from Jan Smuts Airport, Jo'burg, to Heathrow.'

'A single consignment?'

Blake nodded. 'It's an annual shipment. The largest of its kind in the world. The stones are sent cut and uncut to the Diamond Corporation in Charterhouse Street. They're sighted there, and then flown on to New York. The House of Diamonds buys most of them for resale.'

Bart leaned backwards and selected a tattered paperback from a pile on a trolley. The cover showed a pre-war burglar complete with cloth cap, swag bag and mask.

'Ve-ry int-er-est-ing, as they say in these works of literature I dispense. Only how are we to get hold of these diamonds? And what do we do with them even if they can be snatched?'

Blake took the book from him and put it on the counter. 'That,' he said crisply, 'is what *you're* going to tell *me*.'

CHAPTER SIX

Bart asked for a week in which to consider the project; to feed the details into his built-in computer, estimate what he called 'the win/lose percentages', and decide whether or not the Big Job could be done. 'You can go it alone,' he told Blake, 'and recruit your own firm in here. But without that mystic something, you'll never pull a stroke. What this caper needs is star quality, a gimmick, bezazz. That's what I'll either provide, or else forget you ever propositioned me.'

So, for the next few days, Blake kept clear of him and carried his hands around as if they were wounded puppies. The way he saw it at least four people were needed to handle each aspect, development and juncture of the coup. Himself with his inside knowledge; Bart, with his off-centre genius; a muscle man; and someone, a wheel, who could finance the job – put up a short-term loan with unlimited interest.

It had taken him almost his full sentence to find the men needed. In the nick, however, there were two things the cons are rarely short of: ideas for making money illegally, and the right sort of bad companions to help them achieve this.

Blake appraised the two with whom he shared his peter – a dank concrete box, measuring some thirteen feet by seven which had originally been intended for one man. The athlete, whom some sixth sense told him was essential to his scheme, was a narcissist who spent most of his spare time staring into a pool of self-conceit. Known to the cons as the Duchess, his given name was Michael Clancy, a Cockney safe-breaker with cornflower eyes and hair that fitted his head in a skullcap of banana-yellow curls so tight that despite his constant efforts no comb would penetrate it. Aged only twenty-five, he had spent ten years of his life in one kind of institution or another. He was interested in only two things: making money as quickly and dishonestly as possible, and slipping a length, as he put it, to as many as two or three girls a day.

'I was born with this itch between me legs,' he told Blake proudly. 'It's a disease, like some blokes got cancer or TB. I was born itchy and I've been scratchin' meself ever since.'

As with Bart and Blake, Clancy was due for release within the coming three months. He had nothing to go out to except a repeat of all the strokes he'd pulled before – and the jobs that hadn't been successful and had landed him inside. Providing the cash and the sex opportunities were right, he would agree to whatever anyone suggested. But Blake didn't mention anything at first, and reviewed the case of Arnold Monkton, who occupied the top bunk.

Monkton – a twisted-up, scorpion-like figure – said little and brooded a lot. Whenever he was with him Blake avoided the man's shrivelled black eyes and pallid skin which resembled two raisins stuck in lard. The remains of his oily hair was brushed forward and decorated his narrow forehead like a parade of slugs. A long, pock-marked nose stuck accusingly out above a mouth like lemon peel and a boneless, cut-away chin.

A blag merchant from 1945 onwards, from the Black Market of post-war London to the current crime syndicates, he had more payroll robberies to his discredit than most citizens have impure thoughts. He pointed guns the way other people point fingers, and although he hadn't actually killed anyone it was not for want of marksmanship. Twice, he boasted, only the brilliance of surgeons had saved him from being topped.

Experience of really hard nicks had given him the escape bug. But apart from general resentment, he had another, more immediate reason for wanting out. The loot from his last job, an estimated £35,000 snatched from a wages' van in Kilburn High Road, had still not been recovered by the police. His split of that was around seven thousand, sufficient to pay for Blake's caper and still have enough left over for emergencies and the unforeseen.

'It doesn't worry me none to have sat out five years in this craphole,' he muttered in his flat North Country monotone. 'My capital is safely invested and bringing in a juicy return. Better than playing the sodding Stock Market, it is.'

Even so, he knew that no amount of stolen money was ever that secure. And that it only needed someone to grass by telephone or anonymous letter and his 'savings' would be confiscated for good.

These, then, were the men who would form the core, the necessary basic components, of Blake's team. He knew from his Army experience just how important it was not to give a unit too much information about a sortie too soon in advance. Time to think about it allowed doubts and fears – some imaginary, some real – to set in which would end in the failure of the mission and the death of those engaged in it.

So until word came from Bart, he treated his cellmates as he always had done, with mockery, tolerance and reserve. He was aware that they considered him superior. But neither of them challenged the authority he displayed over them, tried to reduce him to their level or offered to fight him in the showers. He imagined they would have liked to have done so, but their instincts told them there was something lethal about him; a fact he'd kept hidden from Karen, and disguised from himself.

During the war he had actually enjoyed killing; had obtained a keen, almost sexual excitement from it. He had never known or looked for the sensation since. But it was there inside: a forbidden, unholy appetite that could return at any time and destroy him, and all those near him, with its lust.

Despite the tension that blocked his windpipe, nothing significant happened until the sixth day after his conversation with Bart. It was seven in the evening, and he'd left the television room before the start of the prison's most popular and admired programme, *Z Cars*. He padded along the ground floor, under the heedful eye of the screw patrolling the balcony, and the sagging, rusted 'suicide' wire which acted as a kind of trampoline if ever people jumped from the upper levels. His cell was on the corner at the end of the first row and he entered it unhurriedly, noting the three bunks stacked like a children's sleeping structure on the right; the table, two chairs and short-legged stool that were its total furnishings; the shallow triangular washstand; the plastic chamber-pots; the naked forty-watt bulb screwed to the ceiling; the barred window the size of a dishcloth which he could reach only by standing hands-stretched and on tiptoe.

He saw Clancy first of all – all bulging muscles and biceps – lying on the lower bunk in the advanced lotus posture, which did things for his abdomen and back. For a moment, he didn't spot Monkton. Then his eyes grew as used as they ever did to the cellar-like gloom. He saw him already under his blanket, his mouth opening and closing as he breathed, like a goldfish's pressed against its bowl.

Clancy lowered his legs and turned on his side towards Blake.

'Got somethin' for you, Phil,' he said, feeling beneath his cardboard-thin mattress and pulling out a twist of paper. 'A stiff from your sweetheart.'

Blake accepted the letter and opened it expectantly, as though it was a motto in a Christmas cracker. He could tell by the broad, backward-sloping writing that it was from Bart. The message it contained would have meant nothing to anyone but him.

Diamonds, it said succinctly, are trumps.

CHAPTER SEVEN

The following morning was Sunday – day of partial rest – and Blake intercepted Bart as they made their way to church from late breakfast. Physically sustained, they were next to receive spiritual nourishment which meant an hour-long sermon from the Reverend E. Stephen Hart who, it was rumoured, was paid by the head for each person who attended his services. Blake jostled against the older man as they filed from the recreation hall and said nonchalantly:

'I got your stiff. We'd better discuss it.'

Bart nodded. 'Church is as good as anywhere.'

'Back row?'

'At the side.'

'A firm of four?'

To his relief Bart dipped his head. Their thinking was on parallel lines.

'The ones I'm threed-up with will do.'

'We need muscle and money.'

'Between them they've got it.'

'Don't let on more than you have to.'

'Don't worry. I've tickled them so far, that's all.'

There were two ways of reaching the chapel, from the inside of the wing and in through a side door or by marching across the exercise yard and going through the keyhole-shaped porch. The side door was for the private use of the Charlie Chaplin, so the men trailed separately into the yard joining a mute crocodile which seemed to have a middle, but no beginning or end.

At first, as he smelt the charred smoke drifting in from the bonfires on the swamps, it seemed to Blake as if they had never left the cells. There was no wind to revive them, to slap them in the face, and the April sun was no more than a puddle reflection.

Then there came a puttering sound quickly louder and nearer and an army helicopter, a five-seater Westland Scout, blew sideways across their heads. It reminded him of a giant dandelion clock; the kind he had told the time on as a kid by blowing away the fruits, an hour for each breath.

Heads lifted to watch its busy progress, then sank again as the chopper flitted over the outer wall and made for the military camp six miles inland. Aircraft from there passed over several times a week, but the cons never failed to react to them like schoolchildren who watch the same trains go by the same windows at the same time each day.

They neared the chapel and Blake forgot about everything except ensuring that he wasn't manoeuvred into one of the front pews. The building itself was made of locally-quarried stone, sand-coloured and peppered with grey like the suit of a country squire. Once inside the nave, the light was transformed by the stained-glass windows to a sub-aqueous greeney blue, still and shadowy as the water in a fish-tank.

He made for the rear pew and reached it to find the three members of his firm sitting there as fixed and graven as book-ends. He grinned at them, squatted on the pew, and raised his arms sideways. His hands were itching under their bandages, and he scratched at them with his chin. The flesh was healing and he felt encouraged by the growth and new life.

Suddenly he saw the Reverend Hart appear behind the ornate, gold lectern. Even before he started to speak, the clergyman's jaw flapped forward so that his sharp grizzled head extended beyond his feet. He had the habit of pulling down the corner of an eye, as if trying to dislodge some dirt that was there.

'Looks as though someone nicked the lead fr'm his roof,' whispered Clancy hoarsely. 'No wonder we're all bloody 'eathens nowadays.'

Hart cleared his throat like an old lady asking the way to the toilet. He then spooned-out the opening driblets of his force-fed piety.

'For my lesson today,' he whinnied, 'I will take the Book

of Isaiah, greatest and most important of the prophets, who in the days of Manesseh suffered death by being sawn asunder . . . . I would like to read to you first of all from Isaiah, forty-nine.'

His voice drooped and saddened as he quoted:

'"*I said to the prisoners, 'Go free',*
and to those in darkness, 'Come out and be seen.'
They shall find pasture in the desert sands
and grazing on all the dunes.
They shall neither hunger nor thirst;
for one who loves them shall lead them
and take them to water at bubbling springs.
I will make every hill a path . . ."'

Blake let him become hypnotized by his own cadence, before turning to Bart and the others.

'Lean forward,' he hissed. 'Pretend you've seen the light.'

They did so, turning themselves into an entity with one body and four heads. No-one around as much as blinked at them, and Blake spoke low and rapidly, as if through a crack in a door.

'You all know what we're here for. What I propose and the roles I want each of you to play. There can only be one boss in this caper, and that's me. It's my idea, and without my privileged information there isn't any job to discuss. Do you all agree to that? If not shout out now while you're still uncommitted. Any voice raised against me after this and it's mutiny and will be dealt with as such!'

He waited for a response to his old-fashioned phraseology and words. Except for Bart, they were 'other ranks' material and must be disciplined accordingly. Monkton, as Blake knew he would, was compelled to quibble.

'That's all very fine for you. But what about us if the job goes sour, or you get nabbed or shot. Who takes over the number one spot?'

'Two things, Monkton, you'd better understand right now. First, the job is *not* going to go sour. Second, and more importantly, there'll be no shooting for the simple fact that we will all be unarmed.' He waited for him to grimace, then went on: 'You can forget about your shooter right now. This is a modern job done by modern non-violent methods. If you want to have a shoot-up, find some death-in-the-afternoon drinking club in Soho, and fire at yourself in the bar mirror. OK?'

'All right,' Monkton allowed grudgingly. 'It's all nineteen canteen.'

'Then see it stays in the past, and don't try reviving it.'

'Thing I don't un'erstand, Phil, is this.'

'Yes, Mike?'

'This tomfoolery you're on about—'

'The diamonds.'

'—how do we snatch 'em? I mean do we hijack the'plane, grab 'em at the airport, or what?'

Blake didn't know that himself yet, but didn't want them to suspect it. He glanced at Bart, whose nod gave him the go-ahead.

'You get two answers for one asking,' he replied. 'If anything should happen to me, then Bart will take my place. If I'm unavailable or you can't locate me, you take your orders from him. If something cancels out the two of us, then the job will automatically be off. Right?

'The rest of the briefing,' he continued, 'I'll leave to Bart. So you get used to his say-so.'

After making sure the clergyman was still delivering and redeeming the people of Israel, Bart spoke in short emphatic bursts.

'Heed you this,' he said. 'Hijacking is out, airport hold-ups are out, tunnelling into vaults is out. The way we get these stones is in transit – while they're still in the air – somewhere between Johannesburg and London.'

Monkton cut in bluntly. 'But that *means* hijacking, don't it?'

Bart wobbled his head; it looked as if the dome was about to fall off St Paul's.

'Not the way we'll do it.'

'And how's that?' Blake was surprised to hear his own voice put the question.

'By the use of two weapons. LSD – the drug, not old money – and an even more potent compound. Mike here and his well-known aphrodisiac effect upon young and nubile women. Particularly those garbed in the uniform of air stewardesses.'

'Do you mind,' said Clancy. 'I never even finished proovy.'

'The two p's,' replied Bart enigmatically. 'Pot and, to use a common vulgarism, your prick, lover-lad.'

'Any time.'

'That's all there is to it?' demanded Monkton.

'All you need know for now. The less you're aware of the less you can divulge.'

'That's no security.'

'I promise you, Arnold, it's a million.'

'Because it's been done before?'

'On the contrary. No job has *ever* been done like this before!'

'Sounds likely.'

'There's only one more factor, the most necessary of all. The loot, the cash, the wherewithal to finance the venture. Without at least five thousand available quid, we might as well resign ourselves to the small time now.'

'Wondered when you'd get round to me specific like,' grunted Monkton.

'Remember,' Blake urged, 'it's a four-way split of three million give or take a rand or two.'

'A *what*?'

'South African for lolly.'

There was a silence so prolonged, so keen, so total that the sermon bleated around them, as insistent as a railway station announcement.

'We will now turn to hymn number 165 in *Hymns Ancient and Modern*,' said Hart optimistically. '"O, God our help in ages past, our hope for years to come".'

The congregation stood as a small console organ trilled an introduction. The organist paused, Hart lifted up his arms, everyone breathed in.

'Done,' said Monkton heavily. 'But you'll have to wait on us. Till after I've done m'bird.'

Blake's agreement was carried away by the first rush of the hymn, was torn from him, thrown to the rafters and bounced there, brought down and sent reverberating round the untapestried walls. He didn't understand all that Bart had said, and didn't need to. The very fact the older man was satisfied, satisfied him.

CHAPTER EIGHT

As Blake's day of release drew nearer, he noticed he was physically and mentally changing. He thought of sex as a two-way process again, requiring a partner, free and female. He now lived at an accelerated pace and experienced things not as a film run in slow motion, but speeded up by an unseen and despotic operator.

He first observed this on the way to a meeting in the library, when an almost forgotten bounce came back to his step, and he found himself trotting instead of snailing along. Clancy was present at the time, and the Cockney warned him about the dangers involved to all of them in the firm.

'It's gate fever,' he said. 'Next thing that happens you'll be pickin' fights. Accusin' your mates of narkin' on you. Sussin' your wife of being charvered by the milkman. Before you know it, you'll be in again before you're out.'

Blake and Bart were due to leave in the same week, with Clancy getting out a week earlier. Their plan was to keep in touch but stay apart until Monkton was set free. But despite the brainwashing session they had with him, the Yorkshireman refused to reveal where his money was stashed, or allow them to use some of it to set the operation up.

'I've got seven g where neither the fuzz nor the villains can touch it,' he stated. 'I'm not as green as I'm bilious-looking.'

'What do you mean – villains?' Blake asked.

'Who do you think is threatening my wife and kids? The law? Don't make me laugh! It's a bunch of the boys who've been round to see them with razors for calling cards. "Where's the loot?" they want to know. "Tell us or we'll use your face as a strop".'

Blake spoke to him more kindly.

'I didn't even know you were married.'

'I'm not any more. The missus is divorcing me. Six years is a long time to spend alone in a double bed.'

His tone was so bitter, so certain that Blake had a quick vision of Karen – her eyes closed and mouth panting open – squirming beneath someone, taking her pleasure wantonly and thinking of him as she came.

'Let me give you a wrinkle,' went on Monkton. 'When this job is pulled find yourself a safe slaughter. Keep the earnings there till the heat's off. It's the only way to stay out of stir.'

'He's right,' said Bart. 'We'll convert the diamonds and bank the money abroad. In a numbered account in Switzerland. It's easily enough done.'

'How?' Blake asked curiously.

'All you need is a minimum of fifty thousand Swiss francs to open an account. That's about £4,750. The interest rate is nothing to rave about. But if you leave your deposit for three months it'll bring in a clear four percent.'

'You mean legitimate money?'

'Either or. Much of it is stolen.'

'How much?'

He shrugged his lips. 'According to the Swiss bankers, none of it is. The United States Treasury tells a different tale. It claims there's an illicit six thousand million dollars in numbered accounts. And that the number of numbered accounts opened by Americans is around the thirty thousand mark.'

'That shouldn't bother us none,' interrupted Monkton.

'No, but what America does today we usually do tomorrow. The Yanks have already put a stop on international credit transfers. Anyone shifting more than five thousand dollars abroad has to report it to the Internal Revenue Department. But it's mainly the Mafia they're after, not the small independents.'

'That's settled, then,' snapped Blake. 'But there's still the problem of disposing of the diamonds. Finding the right fence or buyer.'

'Worry not,' said Bart smiling. 'I've already met that bridge and crossed it. We don't negotiate the diamonds at all. There's no-one in England or Europe we can trust. Take three millions-worth of stones to anyone in London or Amsterdam, and they'll either show you the door or grass to the filth. They don't want to be treated for first-degree burns.'

'So what do we do?' asked Monkton suspiciously. 'Play marbles with them?'

Bart's smile broadened so that his pumpkin head seemed to have been sliced in two.

'We give them back again.'

Blake glanced at the library doors to make sure no one was leaning against them, ready to enter the minute he was seen.

'Give them back?' he repeated. 'Who to?'

'Whoever has the most to lose.'

'The airline?'

'Be sensible. The head of the insurance company.'

'I'm sorry, Bart,' he frowned, 'I'm not with you.'

'Then let me spell it out. You say the stones are insured for their full value – three million pounds?' Blake nodded. 'We can't realize that or anything like it for them. So what we do is this. One of us takes the stones in a velvet bag to the chief of White Star. He shows this man a sample – two or three for proof – and then offers to exchange them, and the rest, for half their insured value. A simple swop which has been done with insurance companies before, and will will be done again. By us, for instance.'

Blake didn't reply, was glad when Monkton raised his standard objection.

'One and a half million sobs is hardly three.'

'No, but it's a lot more than nothing. And nothing is what we'll wind up with if we don't do it my way. What do you say, Phil?'

'Sounds practical enough,' Blake agreed. 'As long as the person you're dealing with doesn't give you away.'

'How can he? Our representative will not admit he's an actual member of the firm. He is only the agent, an intermediary, who's been hired to arrange the deal.'

'Petersen might go for that.'

Bart looked at him quizzically.

'You say you didn't meet him Phil?'

'Never. I was too unimportant.'

'And he works in Cape Town?'

'At the home office.'

'That makes your job all the easier, then.'

'Job. What job?'

'Posing as the agent. Who else among us could do it? Mike? Arnold here?'

'Not us,' put in Monkton. 'When it comes to talking m' foot is seldom far from m'mouth.'

Blake smiled wryly. 'That leaves only me!'

'I'd do it myself,' hastened Bart. 'But you've got to remember two things about me. One, I'm known to the authorities, with a record up to here.' He clamped his left arm at the elbow. 'And two, I have *angina pectoris*. I could live to be a hundred, or I could snuff it at any time. I can just see myself, my blood vessels in spasm, slumped across Petersen's desk inhaling amyl nitrate. . . . It has to be you Phil or no-one.'

The other man spread his hands.

'Okay, Bart. If that's how you want it.'

'You won't regret this, any of you.'

Blake hoped not. For Karen's sake and the boys'.

CHAPTER NINE

A week later after having his mug-shots taken for Interpol and the Criminal Records Office at Scotland Yard Blake was told to report without escort to the governor. He was to receive his 'passing out' talk, and he strode purposefully through the exercise yard, past the governor's garden with its spruce, crew-cut lawn and knob-like flowers and into the Hansel and Gretel house containing the governor's study and private quarters.

Once inside everything turned dark brown and Gothic. Along an oak-panelled corridor with shields, crossed swords and Dutch pictures on the walls. Up to a door with an array of buttons to the side of it, similar to those in a lift. As he'd been told to, Blake pressed the middle button and a yellow light showed on the panel saying, 'Wait'. Soon the light changed to green: 'Enter'. He did so into what reminded him of the smoking room of an old-fashioned provincial hotel. Square leather armchairs that sagged in the middle; balding velvet curtains the colour of uncooked liver; a writing desk in lustreless mahogany, the blotting-paper looking as if moths had been at it.

Behind the desk sat a man some five years older than himself, thick silver hair brushed back without a parting. His nose was hooked the way a hammer toe is, and his blue, washed-out eyes should have been looking down the sights of a rifle, and not into Blake's. Standing beside him was a younger and less well-endowed figure, his lean, hollow face that of a failed but undefeated revolutionary. The governor glanced at a folder open on his desk; fiddled with a gold signet-ring on his left little finger.

'Well now, Blake,' he said breezily. 'Seems that we're getting rid of you. I won't say "at last", as you've spent a mercifully brief time with us.'

Long enough, Blake thought sourly.

'We were wondering, Mr Rudkin and I – he's our probation officer, by the way – what plans you have made for your . . . re-entry into the world.'

A laser beam of light came through one of the diamond panes in the window behind him. Blake blinked and dropped his gaze to the governor's blue-and-red striped, Guards officer's tie.

'I have a wife, home and family to go back to.'

'Capital. No problems there, I take it? Nothing Mr Rudkin can help or advise on?'

'Nothing at all.'

'Excellent.'

There was an embarrassed, three-way silence. Still revolving his ring, the governor gave a smile of encouragement and equality. That, Blake decided, was what he objected to about him. He was giving him the old boys' act . . . you and I are (almost) cut from the same cloth. There but for the grace of good breeding stand I.

He conveyed this without saying a word. Then he again referred to the file.

'Army record first-class . . . decorated and mentioned in dispatches. Nothing but plus marks there.'

He turned a page and went on quoting aloud.

'See you were a member of SIS; most invaluable experience that. Don't you agree, Mr Rudkin?'

'What exactly was your work concerned with?' asked Rudkin distastefully.

'Disinformation,' Blake replied.

'Disinformation?' repeated the governor, the ring spinning round his finger.

'Spreading false propaganda and forged documents. It's aimed at confusing enemy counter-intelligence, and creating general political unrest. And scandals.'

'Ah, yes,' said the governor knowingly. 'The Old Firm.'

'As the diplomats call it.'

'Which brings us to what Mr Rudkin has to say to you. About your future employment. You must have some qualms about that, surely?'

'One thing's certain. I can't go back into DI6 again. Or insurance.'

Rudkin moved forward as if frightened his words wouldn't otherwise carry.

'According to your dossier, you spent four years with White Star in London.'

'Four lifetimes.'

'Quite. So what you are looking for now is something more active and out-of-doors. Responsibility that calls for brawn as well as brains.'

'That's a fair description. What had you in mind?'

'We've been rather fortunate in this,' said Rudkin. 'It's not every case that can be so perfectly matched. I've been in touch with Consolidated Instruments at Slough – they manufacture lubricating machinery. And they have an opening which might have been made for you. In fact, the job is yours for the say-so.'

Blake felt obliged to show interest.

'What kind of job?'

Rudkin made the announcement impressively.

'Security guard.'

Without stopping he went on about pay, uniform, special allowances and pension. Blake would have guffawed, only he didn't want to annoy them. As it was, Rudkin and the governor were hurt and puzzled when he turned their offer down. They couldn't understand his lack of gratitude, the cavalier disregard he had for his wife and dependants.

'Sure you won't change your mind, Blake?' asked the governor before dismissing him.

'Positive, sir.'

'Pity. Then I hope, in the nicest possible way, that we don't meet again.'

'No more than I do, sir.'

As they'd told him, he was released at eight o'clock the next morning. He wore the same tan herring-bone suit in which he'd been sentenced. His personal effects and belongings were bundled into a brown paper parcel, which was handed to him cautiously, as if it contained a severed head. The officer on the gate wished him good luck, and told him to check that he had his railway voucher; a single second-class ticket to Liverpool Street, London and then on to Chislehurst, the nearest station to where he lived in Kent.

Seen from the outside, the main gate and walls of Manston resembled a travel poster version of an English castle. The gate itself was divided into a series of maroon-painted squares, with an arched grille set above them. On each side of this were vertical slits through which arrows could have been fired. The Latin inscription, *Parcere Subjectis* – Mercy for the Vanquished – was carved deep in the iron-grey stone.

He walked briskly downhill towards the village, a drab semi-circle of shops, pub, church, working men's club and school, which appeared to have been dumped there during the last century, and neglected throughout this. He didn't look back and ignored the few people about who glanced at his parcel knowing him for what he was, as if he were a leper with his bell. It was only as the train neared London that he forced his belongings into his pockets, squashed up the paper, and threw it from the open carriage window.

Suddenly he felt very clean.

PHASE TWO

CHAPTER TEN

He spent as little time as possible in London, which he had always disliked because of its size, congestion, noise, dirt and speed. A gobbled pork-pie and hastily swallowed lager in the Liverpool Street buffet, and he was ready to move down to the leisurely space and freshness of the green belt. It was strange at first, being in a mob and yet not a captive part of it, one number among many. Despite the discord and frenzy of the station, he found that no one tried to deliberately crowd him as they had done at Manston.

The people who did bump into him said 'sorry' or 'excuse me', and he knew he'd have to reaccustom himself to politeness and concern. He took the Underground across the centre of the city to Charing Cross, and sat with his arms loosely folded and fingers slack. His only moment of discomfort came when he went to the lavatory in the station, and saw a huge, lumbering, red-haired man approaching. He looked fat and slightly out of condition, but still capable of throwing the average person to the ground. He stopped the moment Blake did and looked apprehensively at him. It took three seconds for Blake to realize it was himself he was gazing at, full-length and unfamiliar in a mirror.

It was mid-afternoon when he reached his destination, and he was the only person to disembark from the train. He handed in his ticket glancing contemptuously at the collector's officious blue uniform and sauntered out into the station forecourt, crammed bumper-to-bumper with the commuters' saloons.

To his satisfaction, Karen was waiting for him with the Renault. He'd been prepared to take a bus on to Brackley, and was pleased that she'd saved him that particular anti-climax. Not that arriving in his wife's inelegant, fawn-painted, box-on-wheels was the most triumphant of returns. But what did he want anyway? Ticker tape, bunting, speeches and cheering crowds?

As she invariably did when driving, Karen had wound

down the nearside window, and he could see her reflection in the mirror on the wing. He walked towards her with the long stride of someone disguising the fact he was in a hurry, noticing the menthol cigarette she held upwards between thumb and two fingers, the long curved-under nails daubed Venetian red, so smooth and glistening they could have been made of plastic. She was chic, cool, sophisticated: everything the fashion magazines she subscribed to said she should be. She saw him loping forwards and their eyes clinched like magnets in the mirror.

'Hello,' he said quickly, wanting to be the first to speak. 'It was good of you to come.'

He bent and kissed her on the corner of her mouth.

'I had to collect the boys. It was no trouble.'

''lo Daddy,' said a smaller, thinner, brighter voice.

A three-year-old head appeared from behind the driving seat capped with marmalade-coloured hair, fringing eyes like blue rosettes.

'Hello, Ian.'

'Where did you been, Daddy?'

'Away on business.'

'I thought you was in hostipal.'

'No, I haven't been sick.'

'I has.'

He moved round to the passenger door, opened it and folded himself in next to Karen. The reason he had bought the Renault was because of its floor space, which was flat and broad enough to stow his legs. Even so, his knee knocked against hers, and he shivered at the sight of her exposed, silk-clad thigh.

'What's been wrong with you, son?'

'I had weasels. Had to go to hostipal.'

He looked enquiringly at Karen. 'You didn't tell me about it.'

She flicked the ignition key.

'He's lying.'

'Telling fibs, you mean.'

'Same difference.'

The car eased ahead and he saw that there was more distance between them than a continent and an ocean.

'Can I have a wice-cream?' asked the voice in the back.

Karen noiselessly changed gear and sent the car zipping

up the hill that led away from the station, towards the commuter village of Brackley, which ten years previously had been a wooded common.

'I thought you had a tummy ache,' she said, keeping her eyes on the road. 'And weren't feeling well.'

'I has. A wice-cream will make me better.'

'Then ask Daddy. He's in charge of things now.'

'Can I, Daddy? Please.'

'Later on. When we get home.'

'Not going home. Going for Lalastair.'

'Oh, whereabouts?' he asked Karen.

'St Peter's. I told you in my letters. He's five now and goes to a proper school.'

'I know. I hadn't forgotten, I just—'

'Didn't remember.'

They left Chislehurst behind them, and entered a tidy plateau of flats, maisonettes and privately-owned bungalows. They went by a church (The First Church of Christ) which looked like a prefabricated factory, and a factory which resembled a country club with its green felt lawn, potted shrubs, and driveway of red and grey gravel. The school was situated at the end of a narrow row of terraced houses left over from the Edwardian era. A congress of mothers had already assembled by the low, wire gate and were talking in groups of three and four like the women one sees pictures of at mining disasters, waiting at the pithead for news. Karen parked the car between a German and English competitor, jutted her elbow from the window and smoothed imaginary lines from her forehead.

'It's hot!' she complained. 'We should have splashed out on a convertible.'

'This school,' Blake said tactfully. 'Is it a good one?'

She shrugged and wrinkled her nose.

'Same as most of the State-runs. Strong on sex education and religion. Weak on the three R's.'

'Alastair can't read or write yet?'

'Nor do his sums.'

'Well, he is only just five.'

'The ones twice his age are little better. They know all about propagating the species, but can scarcely spell their own names.'

It was hot in the car – hot, sticky and uncomfortable. Blake fingered the inside of his collar.

'Sorry I can't afford a private education for them. Not yet anyway.'

She looked at him sideways.

'Is that a hint things might get better?'

'Bound to.'

'Because, as the song says, they can't get worse.'

'Has it been tough on you, financially?'

She thought for a moment.

'No. There's a very discreet pawn shop in Belgravia patronized by all the upper crust and gentry. Whenever the cupboard was bare I simply drove up there and popped my best friends.'

'The diamonds your father gave you?'

'They've fed us before. And probably will have to again.'

'Not this time, Karen.'

'What do you propose using for money: Monopoly notes?'

'Are we that hard-up?'

'Right now we'd qualify for a memorial bench on the embankment. Karen and Philip Blake and family slept here.'

'*Daddy!*'

He saw his father through the windscreen and came charging along the pavement, his head lowered like that of a young bull, his auburn hair flying out behind him as if it was a cape he had thrown over his head. The satchel on his right shoulder made him slightly lop-sided, and his socks were down around his ankles like a footballer with cramp. Blake leaned back and opened the rear door. The boy plunged into the car, hair, satchel, feet, arms, legs going in every direction. He put his arms around Blake's neck, half embracing, half throttling him.

'Now, Alastair,' reproved Karen. 'Daddy's just got back and is tired. Don't make a nuisance of yourself.'

'He's not,' Blake protested. 'He's just happy.'

'What was South Africa like, Daddy?' shouted Alastair. 'When are *we* going there? Did you see Grandpa? Did he give you anything for us? Have you brought presents?'

'Daddy can't speak while you have him by the throat like that.'

'Sorry, Daddy.'

Alastair's fists opened and fell away. But the hands remained on Blake's shoulders and he felt breath coming warmly and moistly on the back of his neck. It was funny about the boys – their colouring and the way they looked. Physically, there seemed to be nothing of Karen in them. They were all his, as if he'd been unfaithful to her and had them by another woman, a mistress as florid and robust as himself.

'I haven't anything for you just now,' he said, and saw their faces lengthen. 'But there *are* presents. They're coming by rail from London.'

'By rail!' exclaimed Alastair. 'They must be super, very big.'

'C'loss'l,' agreed Ian.

Karen drove off again, and they chatted spiritedly on the way home as if there had never been a parting.

'Mummy took us to the zoo,' said Ian presently.

'Really?' Blake replied. 'What did you see there?'

'Cocodriles and things.'

'How exciting!'

'They had very big mouths,' put in Alastair.

'All the better to eat you with.'

'We were quite safe. They were behind bars. Like people in prison.'

For a moment, Karen and Blake locked eyes again. The boys couldn't know about him. No-one would be stupid or cruel enough to tell them! However, the rest of the drive lost its carnival quality, and a robot took over and spoke and acted for him.

Carlton Close, the cul-de-sac they lived in, lay behind a hilly public park and to the side of a tree-ringed, ornamental lake. It was within easy driving range of a small complex of laundrettes and supermarkets; and although there was no cinema or theatre nearby, there was a bingo hall for the women who were housewives and not retired career girls, and a members'-only casino where a tennis club had once stood. The street itself was U-shaped, and contained some thirty pseudo-Georgian houses, all joined together, with a band of communal garden running along the front of them. White was the sole choice of brick, and even the contrasting doors – pink, yellow, lime-green, and violet –

repeated themselves at every fifth or sixth entrance. Brass coach-lamps and lanterns with gold bubble-glass hung from several porches, and the houses themselves had names such as Prinny's, Fitzherbert, The Pavilion, and Beau's Repose.

Their house, The Dome, was on the bend at the right. Karen urged the car off the road, through a gap in the grass, into the garage which occupied most of the ground floor. It was a two-car garage, and they were the only family to have a second car, as it were, without the first. The boys and Blake got out and waited for Karen to repair her face in the rear-view mirror on the dashboard. He held the car door open for her when she'd finished smoothing and patting. She swung her legs and he glimpsed the dark swelling of her pudenda. His throat tightened and he said thickly:

'The house is looking very smart.'

'Let's hope the mortgage company thinks so.'

'Why? Have there been complaints?'

'About the paintwork?' They passed through the side door and into the square steel-and-chrome kitchen. 'No, it's the repayments we haven't made that worry them.'

'How many repayments?'

'Five.'

'Five!'

'As of yesterday. They want their money by the end of the month, or they'll foreclose.'

CHAPTER ELEVEN

It seemed to Blake that night as if the boys would never go to bed. They ate their meal while watching children's television and would only leave the set when the news came on – grave-faced announcements about trouble in Northern Ireland and Vietnam. Karen managed to undress them while they chattered and laughed; but after television they wanted Blake to play with them – hide-and-seek, fighting, a game of Alastair's invention which involved Blake being covered with cushions and jumped upon.

At last they managed to get Alastair upstairs. One second

he was galloping round the room like a racehorse, the next he slumped on the tufted carpet as if brought down. 'The retreat of the walking wounded,' said Karen as she helped him limp away. That left Blake with Ian to contend with, whose energy and verve had not yet reached the point of collapse. With his mother gone, he hid behind the green curtains with the yellow waterlilies on them. 'Don't say where am I, will you?' he begged.

When Karen returned she raised her eyebrows and looked questioningly around. Blake winked and pointed silently to the curtains, beneath which the tips of Ian's toes were showing, pink and delicate as rose petals. She stole forward, plucked him from behind the drapes, and brought him over to kiss his father goodnight.

'Where's Lalastair?' he asked.

'Tucked in and fast asleep already,' Blake replied.

'Did you see him went?'

'Yes, he was very tired.'

'What did you said?'

His eyes closed as if clouds had suddenly obscured a summer-blue sky. Blake kissed him very gently and handed him to Karen. He began to snore, his arms stretched out like signals.

Alone for a while – and how wonderful it was – Blake leaned back on the ochre vinyl couch and parked his feet on the coffee table. He yawned. Perhaps Karen was right, and he *was* tired. When she came back he had grown bored with the blue and red parallels of the Buffet Paris scene above the mantel, and was dozing with his head on one side. She stood over him and ran her hand down his face.

'Wake up,' she said softly. 'It's time to eat.'

He shook himself and looked up at her.

'I wasn't sleeping.'

'You were snoring like the three little pigs in unison. I'm surprised the ceiling didn't fall.'

'Did you mention food?'

'Your favourite. Steak Diane with grilled tomatoes and mushrooms. And a bottle of non-Cypriot wine.'

He stood and wrapped his arms around her. He had to be careful when embracing her. Her skin was dark, but bruised easily.

'I can see you're going to spoil me from now on.'

'Just a little. And just for tonight. Tomorrow the honeymoon is over.'

'Speaking of honeymoons. . . .'

He tilted her head back and kissed her hard, long and deeply. Her body wriggled against his and his hands felt for her small, tight buttocks.

'Not now, Phil,' she breathed. 'The boys aren't properly asleep yet.'

'The way I feel there could soon be an addition to the family.'

'Im-possible.'

'Why? Don't tell me it's—'

'No. I'm perfectly fit and able. I was referring to the Pill – which no reunited wife should be without.'

They moved into the kitchen and he watched her prepare the meal. She handled the dishes, plates and cutlery with the skill and speed of a cardsharp; dealt them out while he wrestled the cork from the wine – a rich, full, chateau-bottled Burgundy. They ate in the dinette by candlelight – two scarlet candles with black wicks, standing beside brandy glasses with a single rose in each. They said little during the meal, but rarely took their eyes off each other, and allowed their feet to flirt beneath the table. By some nocturnal miracle, neither of the boys came down for drinks of water or snacks, and they reached the brandy stage without interruption.

A short while later they took their drinks from the table, and sat together on the couch. There was an evening chill in the air and Blake turned on one bar of the fire. The artificial coals glowed redly at them, the flames seeking a chimney to climb up and escape.

'Shall I help with the washing-up?' he asked when the brandy was finished.

'I think tonight we can leave the dishes in the sink.'

'Ma,' he added.

She smiled, rose, and stretched lazily.

'I'll tell you what you *can* do,' she murmured.

'Name it.'

'Carry me to bed.'

CHAPTER TWELVE

While Blake made a husband of himself again – and a woman of Karen – the man with the hearing-aid sat in an office some six thousand miles away studying a message from an agent in London.

The message had arrived by telex that evening just as the man was leaving his office to eat. He tore the strip of paper from the machine, took it with him as he dined, read it and reread it throughout the meal. He returned to the now darkened skyscraper, set between a mountain and a bay. Once more studied the words that had been teleprinted to him.

BLAKE RELEASED EARLY THIS MORNING (EIGHTEENTH) STOP REUNITED WITH WIFE AND FAMILY STOP DO YOU WISH ENQUIRIES PURSUED STOP PLEASE ADVISE STOP WHITFIELD

For a time the man with the hearing aid watched the light seep from the sky, a cuticle of moon appear. Up until then he hadn't known whether to continue the surveillance or not. Perhaps Karen was right and Blake would be too sensible, too mature to make such a mistake again. But it was the fact that Blake had been caught and imprisoned that worried the man. The former officer and civil servant would never have been so crude, so obvious, so amateurish. Something was wrong, didn't fit the pattern. The man with the hearing-aid knew he must find out where the error lay, what piece had been distorted to complete the picture.

He rose and crossed to the telex machine in the corner of the room. He bent over it and tapped out his reply:

MAKE NO MOVE AND DO NOT SHOW YOURSELF TO SUBJECT STOP CONTINUE DISCREET OBSERVATION STOP REPORT DEVELOPMENTS IMMEDIATELY STOP GOOD WORK STOP

He added his name to the message and left for the night.

A continent to the north of him, Karen and Blake cried out together.

CHAPTER THIRTEEN

'You know what I first liked about you, darling?'

'No. What?'

'The way you look like a Viking. That mane of red hair, and your being so tall and blue-eyed and everything.'

'I bet you say that to all your husbands.'

'Only the Scandinavian ones.'

Karen margarined a second slice of breakfast toast, and adjusted the calorie indicator propped against the silver coffee pot.

'The Viking touch,' she continued thoughtfully. 'And, of course, your sense of humour.'

'Barbed and acerbic.'

'Very mocking and dry. Your public school background, I suppose.'

'Boarding school,' Blake corrected. 'Our principal did *not* attend the Headmasters' Conference.'

'I like the way you mock at life, Phil. It lessens its – intensity.'

'I scoff so that I may not weep.'

'Even so, I like it. Which is more than I can say for that beard you're sprouting.'

His right hand crawled through the air and clutched the growth on his chin.

'It is a bit straggly,' he admitted.

'I hope you're not going native.'

'Hardly. Even in Manston I shaved every day. Besides, I thought all true Vikings had beards. An essential part of their image.'

'It's just that Daphne is coming round for coffee. You could at least look a little less – mangy.'

'Daphne?'

'Daphne Willard. She and her husband got back from holiday last night.' She hesitated over a third piece of toast, consulted her calorie chart, and decided against it. 'I thought you'd prefer not to be here when she arrives.'

'She has a thing about ex-convicts? A strong moral repulsion?'

'Not in the least. I'd like to be able to tell her you were out—'

'Breaking rocks in the garden.'

'– looking for a job.'

He folded his napkin, laid it on his plate, and rose.

'I have to go up to town anyway.'

'To see about work?'

He gestured theatrically.

'Why else do you think I'm growing this beard? To disguise myself from Interpol?'

'Don't be absurd!'

'It's to add to my new-found respectability. That and a pipe, and I'll be salaried again within the month.'

'I'm glad, darling. For your sake.'

He wasn't annoyed at what Karen had said, but her comments upset him. There was a year to go before Monkton was released and would finance the coup. By that time he wanted not only to look different – a beard, sideburns, his hair dyed brown – but to *be* different. Someone who spoke differently, slowly and with reserve. And who moved differently: he must become lighter on his feet, more mobile and smart. Unfortunately, there was nothing he could do about his hands except wear gloves or keep them in his pockets. If the Big Job did go wrong, and they were caught, he didn't want it to be on his account because he was like a walking sore thumb.

He spent the next half-hour combing the unevenness from his beard, forcing himself into a pinstriped City suit that had once fitted him, ringing his insurance manager for an appointment. He planned to placate the mortgage company with money from a life policy he would cash in. He was just about to leave and walk to the station (he also needed to lose weight), when he heard Mrs Willard make a loud, talkative entrance. She was extolling the benefits of suburban Buddhism when he went into the lounge to say goodbye.

'Why, Mr Blake!' she cried shrilly, examining him through rhinestone-studded glasses. 'How good to see you again after all this time.'

'Yes,' he said, moving forward and wagging hands with her. 'It's been at least a year.'

'All of that.'

He smiled down at her, a brittle, dark, gypsyish woman in multi-coloured blouse and peasant skirt.

'I'm just off to London,' he said pointedly. 'I have some business to attend to there.'

'Already!' she exclaimed. 'You *are* a man of righteous action!'

'Very much so. I've had my sabbatical; now it's back on the treadmill.'

'Your wife was just telling me how you plan to start a new karma.'

'Karma?'

'Destiny, or the doctrine of rebirth, as we Buddhists call it. Away with the old life-style and on with the new.'

'Indeed. Well, if you'll both excuse me, I have an appointment to keep.'

He again took Mrs Willard's stick-like hand in his, then went and kissed Karen on the cheek. She was wearing a new kind of powder, and it smelt to him of hotel rooms, mistresses, love in the afternoons.

'I'll be back about five,' he said. 'I'll ring if I'm going to be late.'

'Don't miss the boys' bedtime. You know how they look forward to being with you then.'

'Daddy the human toy.'

'Good luck,' carolled Mrs Willard. 'I shall be meditating for you.'

His business with the insurance company took longer than he'd expected. It appeared that his bank had failed to make two monthly payments while he'd been inside, and there was talk of the policy having lapsed. It took a 'phone call to the bank manager, a cheque, another 'phone call to make sure the cheque wouldn't bounce, before it was grudgingly agreed to let him surrender the policy. He was allowed £500 on it which, as it carried no bonuses, was about what he'd paid in instalments. He left to a frosty goodbye from the manager, emerged onto Ludgate Hill and headed south towards the river, and the offices of White Star.

He didn't really know why he did that. As far as the tomfoolery was concerned, he needn't go near the place until later – when he had to threaten, blackmail or bribe some information from one of his former colleagues. He wasn't certain who it would be, and stood in a doorway opposite the building looking up at the window at which he had formerly worked. He could see the back of someone's head and shoulders, hunched over the desk that used to be his. If he turned round, this engrossed intruder, Blake felt he would see his own face staring down at him.

He moved off just as a man in a flashily checked suit came out of the Kardomah coffee house which acted as an unofficial annexe for the employees of White Star. His face was scarlet and a thick roll of flesh lay like a rope around his neck. His hair was very fair and thin, so that it seemed he was either bald, or an albino. Blake didn't need to look into his watery pink eyes to know that Roy Whitfield had been out for a cup of Blue Mountain coffee, with a miniature bottle of brandy poured in it.

He was the one, when it came to apply the pincers and thumbscrews, who would be led into the chamber. Roy Whitfield raised insurance premiums without anyone but the clients knowing about it and kept the difference for himself. Whitfield's method was so ingenious that when Blake had suspected it, and then used his Government training to break it down, he had done nothing but privately applaud.

Blake held back so that he would not be seen, then walked along the embankment to the foot of Villiers Street, and up to Charing Cross. He mulled over his chance sighting of Whitfield; seeing but not listening to the newsboys outside the station shouting about a 'break'. While not usually superstitious, he felt he had been given a sign, and that the Big Job was more possible and immediate than before.

He pressed the doorbell of The Dome (must get a new key cut for himself) at a quarter to six, and heard the three descending notes that always suggested to him a radio station coming on the air. Karen opened the door as the last chime faded, looked at him as though he'd been away for a month.

'Don't panic,' he said. 'I only stopped in for a beer at The Sun.'

'It's not me who's worried about you. It's your friend who's been on the 'phone all afternoon.'

'What friend?'

'He wouldn't give his name. Just said he had to talk to you urgently.'

Blake edged past her and moved inside.

'What did he sound like, this mysterious caller?'

'Vicious, vulgar and coarse.'

He tried joking it off.

'Possibly someone I met inside.'

'Where else?'

He looked through the lounge door and saw the boys sitting in front of the set as if turned to stone, watching *The Magic Roundabout.*

'Did he leave any message?'

'He told me, in quaintest Cockney, that you must watch the ten-to-six news.'

'The news?'

' "Wifaht file", as he put it.'

CHAPTER FOURTEEN

He picked his way into the lounge, stepping over a new red-and-blue tricycle, bypassing a knee-high model of a London bus that hadn't been there that morning.

'Thank you for the toys, Daddy,' said Alastair, without turning his head from the machine. 'They're smashing.'

'Specially the bus,' added Ian.

'I'm glad you like them.'

He looked questioningly at Karen. Where had they come from? Who had paid for them? And with what?

'Remember, darling,' she murmured. 'The gifts that were coming by train? They finally got here.'

He flushed, realizing he hadn't remembered and that she had gone out and bought them herself. He wondered which item was missing from her jewel-box this time. *The Magic Roundabout* revolved, and Dougal, Zebedee and the rest of the characters spun from sight.

'All right, boys,' said Karen crisply. 'Take your toys up to the playroom. Daddy has something to do in here.'

'Must we, Daddy?'

'I want to watch the news. Off you go now.'

'The news!' said Alastair contemptuously. 'How boring!'

The trailer for a situation comedy programme being shown later that night ended. The boys rode and drove from the room, and Blake stood in front of the set as though he'd been summoned there by it. The energetic, urgent music started; the word NEWS flashed on and off, on and off; a picture of Manston filled the screen. It was a general view, taken from the swampland and looking downhill on the grey stockade of buildings. The image faded, was instantly replaced by the plump face of the newscaster, dark hair gleaming.

'It is now known,' he intoned gravely, 'that two of the three men who broke out of Manston Prison, in Norfolk, this afternoon, have got away. The third man was caught after a scuffle with prison officers in the main street of the village near the prison.

'One of the officers was injured and was later taken to hospital with a suspected fractured skull.

'The two men who succeeded in escaping are Gordon Bates, twenty-one, who was serving an eight-year sentence for armed robbery and Ronald Oates, thirty, who was sentenced last March for ten years on a charge of rape and attempted murder.

'The two wanted men—'

As pictures of Bates whom Blake knew by sight and Oates, a stranger to him, were shown the newscaster spoke solemnly about the means and method of escape. Apparently they had hidden in the back of one of the garbage trucks that visited Manston each Friday. They had been spotted jumping from the vehicle in Manston High Street, and had then encountered a group of off-duty prison officers.

'The third man, Arnold Monkton, forty-seven, also serving a term for armed robbery, was brought to the ground and held down by three of the officers. He was taken back to Manston, and this evening was being transferred to the maximum security wing there—'

A mug shot of Monkton appeared, set-faced and glowering, everyone's concept of a brutal criminal and con.

Before any more was said, Blake strode irritably forward and blinded the set. Karen moved beside him, slipped her arm through his, propped her head against his shoulder.

'Those men on the news,' she uttered, 'the two who are on the run. Are they anything to do with you?'

'With me! Good God, no.'

'Then it must be the other one; the one they caught. What was his name. Mankin?'

'Monkton.'

'What would *you* want with someone who's an armed robber?'

'Nothing, of course. It just so happens that I shared a cell with him. Me and this other fellow, Clancy.'

'The one who was released the week before you?'

'That's right.'

'He's a Cockney, isn't he?'

'He has Bow Bells for testicles.'

'I still don't understand why he should ring *you* up. And be so persistent about it.'

'Probably some kind of instant nostalgia. You can get very attached to the people you're threed up with. Either that or you want to kill them!'

'But how did he know your telephone number?'

'It's in the book. Even Cockneys can read.'

'I know that, Phil. I'm not dense, it's just that—'

Before she could finish, the eau-de-nil telephone in the hall began its nagging. They looked at each other apprehensively, as if a kidnapper was on the line.

'You'd better answer it,' she said. 'It's bound to be your jailbird friend.'

'Do you want to listen in on the extension?'

She flinched.

'I'd rather not know. Whatever it is he's after.'

Blake nodded and walked from the room. The 'phone was still ringing, sounded as though it would never stop. He lifted the receiver and grunted 'Hello'. There was a pause while a coin was inserted. Then Clancy rasped his name.

'You see the news all right?' he asked.

'The bit about Manston, yes.'

'Where was you all afternoon?'

'Out looking for work.'

'Then you needs look no furver.'

'How?'

'Got a message for you from Bart.'
'Go on.'
'He wants a meetin' wiv the free of us.'
'When?'
'Tomorrer.'
'Where?'
'His place.'
'And where might that be?'
'Hold on a tick. I got it written dahn.'
There was a silence and Blake pictured him juggling the receiver and a scrap of grubby paper.
'Got it!' he exclaimed. 'Twenty-six Leinster Crescent, W2. Just offa the Bayswater Road.'
'I know the district.'
'Eleven o'clock prompt.'
'What's it all in aid of?'
'Search me, mate. He just said for you to be there.'
Blake glanced behind him made sure Karen was out of earshot.
'It's something to do with Monkton, isn't it?'
'Dunno.'
'We have to do something about him – or else call the caper off.'
Blake heard a tapping noise, as if Clancy was drumming his nails on the mouthpiece.
'Is anyone listenin' your end?' he said finally.
'No.'
'Then I'll tell yer. Bart says we're gonna spring 'im.'
Blake felt his jaw sag, was still standing there stupefied when Clancy hung up and the buzzing tone rang in his ear.
Spring Monkton?
From a maximum security wing?
They must both be mad!
He re-entered the lounge in a daze. Karen was sitting with her legs tucked under her on the couch. She flipped through the pages of a food and health magazine.
'Well?' she asked, keeping her eyes down. 'Was it all that important?'
He shook his head and came to.
'No,' he said. 'Just another old lag's tale.'

CHAPTER FIFTEEN

Blake left the house early the next morning telling Karen he had to go up to town and see a man about a job. Factually, that was true enough, and he lied to her only in spirit. But she was not content to leave it at that, and asked questions in a lethargic, indifferent way as if the subject was a bore and she couldn't care less about it. Which told him just how interested she was.

'What sort of job?' Her voice a lazy afterthought.

'Tourist guide.'

'You're going to work abroad?'

'In London. Showing Americans around St Paul's, Westminster Abbey, the Tower. Places of historical appeal.'

'And what do you know about historical appeal?'

'Nothing yet. But I can read it up. Besides, the money's not bad.'

'How much is not bad?'

'Twenty pounds a week basic; plus tips.'

'Better than average for you.'

'Of course I haven't landed it yet.'

'And if you don't land it?'

'Then I shan't come home.'

'Is that a threat or a promise?'

'A threat!'

'Sometimes a girl prefers promises.'

After that he didn't kiss her goodbye, and she didn't ask him to.

He felt strange being behind the wheel of the Renault again. It seemed longer than twelve months since he'd last driven, and he had difficulty at first in finding the ignition. He switched on and remembered just in time that the gear positions were the reverse of those on British cars. It wasn't until he entered the southern outskirts of London – Lewisham and the Old Kent Road – that his confidence fully returned. The car stopped its rolling, and he no longer knocked the lights on when changing from second gear to third. He buzzed in and out of the traffic like a lively, impertinent wasp and took the road through Hyde Park to Bayswater.

Soon he turned off the main drag and cruised along the crumbling semicircle of Victorian houses that was Leinster Crescent. Number twenty-six was a blank-faced private hotel – the Tudor Court according to the Gothic lettering on the canopy – and seemed the sort of place where it was not necessary to have luggage. He slotted the car into a line of vehicles that looked as if they had been abandoned rather than parked, and noticed the absence of credit card signs at the hotel entrance.

Inside, through the creaking swing-doors, was a length of footworn carpet, some dusty potted palms, a wedge-shaped reception desk. Behind the desk, bow-chested and stout, stood a woman wearing a tie, monocle, and tweed hacking jacket. Her chin was speckled with moles and her short dark hair was brilliantined and combed back from her forehead. As Blake approached she regarded him hostilely.

'Excuse me,' he smiled 'but I'm looking for a Mr Bartholomew.'

She ran a blunt forefinger down the register.

'Is he a guest here?'

'He gave me this address.'

'That doesn't mean he's staying with us.'

'It doesn't?'

'He could be expecting you in the bar. All sorts walk in here off the street.'

'Then perhaps I could—'

She closed the book with a snap and emerged from her stronghold.

'Legally, the bar is not open yet. But you may go in there and wait.'

'Thank you.'

'Will you be taking luncheon with us?'

'I'm not sure. It depends on—'

'Ask the barman for the menu, and give him your order. Luncheon is from one prompt to two-thirty sharp. The fare is plain but ample. Those desiring Savoy cuisine must pay Savoy prices. The bar is second on the left down the corridor. Tell Max that Miss Ridley sent you.'

She turned dismissively away and invaded a room marked Colour Television Lounge. She began haranguing someone whose outstretched feet he could see, and he followed her directions to the bar. It was as shoddy and uncared-for as the rest of the hotel. A number of green-painted bamboo chairs and couches were pushed back against the wall, and there was more bamboo framing the bar itself, so that anyone standing behind it appeared to be in a coop. The linoleum floor was uncarpeted and of no discernible hue; a large, stationary fan hung from the ceiling like the propeller of a ship. He paused, then heard someone call his name.

'Over here, Philip. In the corner.'

He stepped around a lacquered screen and saw Bart sitting alone at a low glass-topped table. He was wearing a biscuit-coloured lightweight suit, with matching tie, shirt, shoes and socks. An expatriate on leave from the Colonies. Blake sat down and Bart pointed to the drink in front of him.

'Mint julep,' he said. 'Speciality of the house. Shall I get Max to fix one for you?'

'Not before sundown.'

Bart moved the glass about on a cork table mat, making a series of fussy little arcs.

'What do you make of this Monkton business, then?' he said softly. 'Can you imagine anyone being such a clown?'

'It's our own fault,' replied Blake. 'It's something we should have reckoned on.'

'My fault, you mean. I'm the alleged brains.'

'They'll increase his sentence, won't they?'

'They'll do that all right, but not for scarpering. It's no crime to escape from prison. But kicking an officer in the head and fracturing his skull is.'

'What'll it bring him?'

'Another handful.'

'We can't wait five years for him! Another five days is all I can stand with no job and no money.'

'Take it easy, Phil. With luck you won't even have to wait that long.'

'Because you're going to spring Monkton?'

'Because *we're* going to spring him.'

'The three of us?'

'With the help of another.'

'Which reminds me. Where is Bill Sykes junior?'

'Within spitting distance of here. Chatting up the third party I mentioned.'

'Bart?'

'Yep.'

'I've changed my mind. I will have that drink after all.'

Blake sat silently while Bart semaphored to the barman for two more of the same. The drinks came together with trays of potato crisps, cocktail onions and gherkins. Blake sipped what appeared to be sweet mint sauce from a tall glass with pictures of harlequins on it.

'Give,' he said quietly. 'The when, the how, the with whom.'

'The time – approximately this time tomorrow.'

'So soon!'

'Has to be. They've put our friend in Manston maximum security wing, and that's tough enough. But they'll transfer him to a real strongbox by the end of the week. E-Wing at Durham, or Vectis on the Isle of Wight, and you know what that means, don't you?'

Blake counted on his fingers.

'Closed circuit television; electronic alarm devices that are triggered off when anything or anyone comes in sight; chain-link fencing; barbed wire; floodlights – the lot.'

'That's only the half of it. These new nicks are built to withstand an armed military attack. The cells have spring-loaded floors which are wired to a control room. That way an officer can look at his master panel and see exactly what part of the peter the con is actually *standing* in. As long as he stays in the centre of the floor, the panel shows yellow. If he goes to the door it shines green. But as soon as he nears the window, a red light starts blinking.

'Then there's the guard dogs and karate-trained screws to contend with. No, Monkton's had it this time. He's been reclassified category A+, a serious security risk. You'd have to dynamite the prison to get him out!'

'You mentioned armed attack,' prompted Blake. 'Is that how you propose springing him?'

'No. For one thing the guards themselves aren't armed, and for another I've calculated how it can be done rapidly, cleanly, and without bloodshed.'

'And the how and with whom?'

'You'll find that out five minutes from now when we meet old Freddie.'

'Freddie?'

'Freddie Reynolds – without whom Monkton will stay in maximum security until he rots.'

'There's just one more thing. Where do we hide Monkton once he *is* free? The whole of the British police force will be out looking for him.'

Bart smiled like a small boy with a guilty secret.

'Hazard a guess.'

'Any scruffy little bed-sitter will do.'

'Or dubious private hotel.'

'*Here?*'

'Where else? My cousin runs an extremely efficient hide-out. You'd be surprised the big names who've registered with her when they were on the run.'

'Your cousin?'

'Martha Ridley. You must have met her on your way in. No one enters without her running her geiger counter over them.'

He pushed away the remains of his drink and they rose and walked to the corridor.

'If Monkton can't get out to us,' said Blake, 'and we can't get in to him, then how are we going to spring him? By descending God-like from the sky? *Deus ex machina* and all that?'

Bart chuckled and gripped him affectionately by the elbow.

'Know something, Phil? You're getting to act, talk and even think like one now.'

'One what?'

'One category A+ villain.'

CHAPTER SIXTEEN

Outside, Blake noticed how small and mediocre Bart looked in his tea planter's outfit. Except for his eggshaped yellow head, there was nothing outstanding or remarkable about him. In prison that had not been the case: there he had seemed a civilized giant among pygmies. But Manston was a lifetime and a universe away. It seemed he knew no other Bart than the one attempting to keep pace with him now, gasping and wheezing, slipping a small white tablet underneath his tongue.

'Slow down to a gallop,' he said breathlessly as they wheeled left towards Marble Arch.

'Where are we going to, anyway? Blake asked.

'The Wings Club. It's for ex-RAF officers and pilots of all types. The sole qualification for belonging being your ability to fly a plane.'

'Which your friend Mr Reynolds does?'

'Anything and everything – but he specializes in whirlybirds.'

'In what?'

'Choppers. Helicopters; aerial machines that can land on a tenpenny piece, and take off on a five.'

'With Monkton stashed away inside.'

'If he's lucky.'

They reached the junction of Leinster Crescent and a drab street leading to Paddington station. Blake was about to follow the curve, but Bart tugged his arm and ushered him down a flight of dog-dirtied concrete steps and into a basement area. Ahead of them some rusted and overflowing dustbins stood guard beside a door with a Judas eye. A pair of rigidly outstretched wings was painted above the peep-hole and they approached the door through an ankle-deep drift of refuse.

'Here they don't need garbage strikes,' groused Bart, opening the door with his foot. He stood back and waved Blake into a long tunnel-like room, hazy with cigarette and cheroot smoke, with a bar like a shooting-gallery at the end of it. They halted and saw Clancy in a white, belted jacket with pleats up the back sitting next to a jukebox with a small, moustachioed man drinking milk through a straw.

'There's old Freddie,' said Bart softly. 'Back on the cow cart.'

'He's an alcoholic?'

'I would that he were.'

'What *is* his weakness?'

'Horse – taken intravenously, or through the mouth.'

'A junky! We can't possibly trust a junky!'

'We've no alternative. If it wasn't for Freddie's weakness, his eight grammes a day, we'd have no bargaining power with him. What we pay him to fly his chopper, buys him what he needs to fly his chopper, if that isn't too circular for you.'

He shuffled forward and Blake followed him over to the table. The jukebox was playing one of the old records that inexplicably come back into fashion every now and then, a tune 'interpreted' by Spike Jones and his City Slickers and they sat to an accompaniment of hoots, horns, yodels and trombones breaking wind. Blake nodded to Clancy, and shook hands with Reynolds, whose fingers quivered as though currents of electricity were passing through them. He was about the size and weight of a conscientious jockey. His head was heavy with dandruff, the scales lying unbrushed on the lapels and shoulders of his crested, navy-blue blazer. The lower part of his body – grey flannels and cherry-red brogues – was sheathed with cigar ash. Blake felt he needed to be hung out on a clothes-line, and vigorously beaten.

They talked generalities while Clancy went for more drinks, and Reynolds explained why the walls of the club were the colour of French mustard.

'They used to paint the old Sopwith Camels that shade,' he said in a voice that reminded Blake of someone sucking fruit. 'Ever been up in one of those? Pity. Much more spunky than the Hurricanes and Tempests Sir Tommy built later. Mind you—'

He was still reminiscing when Clancy returned and banged another glass of milk before him. It wasn't until Bart had fed the jukebox with enough money to scramble their conversation for an hour, that Reynolds became positive and alert.

'Your goby here has given me the SP,' he said. 'And I don't like it. Not one little bit.'

It was only when he used thieves' and not RAF slang, that Blake realized he had form like the rest of them. Had he been in Manston, or Dartmoor, or the Scrubs?

'I know it's a bit smelly—' agreed Bart.

'A bit!'

'– but that's what we're paying you for. The risks involved and taken.'

'How much are you going to bung me?'

'Down payment? Or later, when we've pulled the job?'

'For openers, how much?'

'A grand.'

Reynolds siphoned some more of his milk, swilled it thoughtfully in his mouth.

'You must be joking. Five grand is the minimum deposit. Plus half your earnings from the job.'

Clancy, who had been studying his reflection in a photograph of a Royal Flying Corps squadron in Salonika, leaned forward and said spikily:

'That sort of loot's for the top boys; the one's what sprung Biggs and Wilson.'

'I couldn't agree more, sonny. If *you* were in their league, and *you* had their kind of loot, I'd be asking for fifty thousand down in crisp new fivers. But you're not the Great Train Robbers, and neither is the man you want sprung! I'll settle for five grand now, and another five once he's safely underground. Take it or leave me alone.'

But Bart would do neither. He spent twenty niggly and exhausting minutes persuading the pilot he'd get a thousand down; another four thousand within a month; the final five by the end of the year.

'It's better than no offer at all,' he concluded. 'And let's face it, who else wants to use you, Freddie? We didn't exactly have to queue-jump to get you.'

The man's whole body twitched as he heard that. He clamped one hand on top of the other on the table.

'All right,' he muttered. 'As long as you understand the dangers entailed. There're only some two hundred qualified private chopper pilots in Britain. Once your man is sprung, the fuzz will interview each and every one of us. I'll need to buy myself an alibi, and then take a business trip abroad.'

'Which you can arrange yourself.'

'Easy as falling from a 'plane.'

'What sort of bus have you got at the moment?'

'A Hughes 200. She's oldish, but she seats three and should be adequate for the job.'

Bart wobbled his head in disagreement.

‘Too small and too civilian. What we have to do is look as much like a Westland Scout as possible.’

‘But that’s an Army plane!’ protested Reynolds. ‘Painted green and brown and used for general purposes and reconnaissance.’

‘That’s what your chopper must look like.’

‘Then ideally I’d need a Jetranger!’

‘Is that so impossible?’ asked Blake.

‘You wouldn’t know it, but a Bell Jetranger costs nearly fifty-five thousand new, second-hand you still get more than forty thousand for them.’

‘Save us the sales talk,’ said Clancy. ‘Can you get hold of one or not?’

‘’Course I can’t. A – if I owned one myself I wouldn’t need the kind of pittance you’re offering. B – no-one’s going to lend me one of those without a lot of unanswerable questions being asked. It’s the Hughes or nothing.’

‘All right,’ agreed Bart. ‘But can you fake her up to look something like a Westland?’

Reynolds nodded.

‘Mine’s grass-green already. Only needs the brown daubed on her. The RAF rings and Army lettering are no sweat.’

‘Will she get you from here to Manston and back?’

‘She has a range of three hundred miles. Should be sufficient.’

‘And is she fast enough in case of pursuit?’

‘Her top speed is a hundred and nine, and she cruises at a hundred. A Brantly B2B has the catching of her, let alone one of the bigger jobs.’

‘But you’ll have at least a head start.’

‘Let’s hope I don’t need it.’

Blake became impatient with the technical chat, told them so in a lull between the music.

‘Relax, Phil,’ said Bart soothingly. ‘This isn’t for my sake, you know.’

‘Then who’s is it for?’

‘Yours.’

‘Mine!’

‘As I told you before, I’m too prone to closed blood vessels to take part in this sort of caper. And Clancy here is short on staying power and guts. He has his uses, and will prove invaluable later on. But right now, Phil, the ball’s in your court. See if you can get it back over the net.'

Another old disc was lifted by the automatic arm and dropped into place in the jukebox. Bing Crosby, in the early days when he whistled and crooned.

'Now that we're agreed in the main principles,' said Bart, augustly tapping his foot, 'let's get down to the nitty-gritty. Just how Philip is going to swing it; what he considers are its chances of success.'

They conferred until they'd called up every record on the machine. There was a silence in which they could have heard a gramophone needle drop. The three men looked at Blake with a single, questioning head.

'Well,' encouraged Bart. 'Is it feasible or a frost?'

'Feasible,' Blake said tonelessly. 'Very feasible indeed.'

CHAPTER SEVENTEEN

'Well, did you get the job?'

'Yes; if I want it.'

'Why so dubious?'

'There's more travelling to it than I thought.'

'So you *will* have to go abroad.'

'Occasionally.'

'The south of France and Spain.'

'No such luck. South Africa, believe it or not.'

'South *Af*rica!'

'This outfit specializes in visitors from there. The head office is in Johannesburg, and I'll have to fly out there sometimes. For briefings, pep talks and general indoctrination, as they termed it.'

'What's it called, this company?

'Home From Home Holidays.'

'Never heard of it.'

'It's new since your time.'

'Did being married to a South African help?'

'Enormously. That's the kind of background they're looking for in their tour guides. I was told to include it in my chat to the visitors: "By the way, my wife comes from Cape Town and she still hankers after mieliepap for breakfast–" Sighs of nostalgia, instant success of Philip Blake.'

'Glad to be of service.'

'Mind you, I'm only on trial as yet. I'm free to sack them, and they're free to sack me.'

'And when does it start, this new career of yours?'

'Tomorrow morning.'

'That's quick!'

'A rush job. I have to meet a plane at the airport. I'll be back when you see me.'

'Philip.'

'Uh-huh?'

'Good luck.'

CHAPTER EIGHTEEN

The airfield Bart told Blake to report to was situated on the north-east fringe of London; somewhere behind and to the right of Epping Forest. It was an area he hadn't visited since his courting 'teens, and he twice got lost as he nosed the Renault through the petrified, moonscape territory. Before reaching Brett Hill, as it was called, he passed two areas with rotting buildings and overgrown asphalt that could have been the Heathrows of their day. It wasn't until the forest was a blur in his rear-view mirror, that he suddenly saw a windsock pointing at him like a long, tapered balloon. Along the sock – in faded blue letters – were the words BRETT HILL FLYING CLUB. A few yards further on he turned off the main road, mounted a rutted cart track and passed through a sagging five-barred gate. He coaxed the car forward onto the asphalt with grass sprouting through the cracks like the hair in a battered sofa, and coasted towards the abandoned control tower.

At the side of the chipped, fawn-painted slab were a lopsided hangar, a mound of derelict machinery, the sort of hut more usually seen on building sites. Parked in the centre of this wasteland was a vintage, open topped Bentley; spinach green, with the bottom hanging from it as though it suffered from piles. It could only have been Reynolds' car, and he wondered if they'd been brought together by computer, they were so perfectly matched.

There was no-one about as he stepped from the car, the

wind snatching spitefully at the roots of his hair. He walked across the crazy-paving of the concrete and tried the workmen's hut. It was empty save for a mug of cold, half-finished tea and a bacon sandwich with a bite taken from it. Ignoring the control tower, he entered the hangar which smelt as if it had been soused with petrol. Three or four cats yowled and ran by his feet. He realized the stench probably came from them; them and the paint which Reynolds was applying to the helicopter, which lay like a tethered glass bubble on the floor of the shed. He stood up as he saw Blake approaching, displayed the pot and brush in his hand.

'Morning,' he said breezily. 'Take a dekko at my brush-work. The Sistine Chapel isn't in it.'

Blake gazed critically at the chopper, thinking that, in the circumstances and the time at his disposal, Reynolds hadn't done too inexpert a job. The aircraft looked little like a Westland Scout; that would have been too perfect to expect. But to the slothful, grown-accustomed eye she would pass for an Army machine. The green and brown stripes were broad and sombre enough, and the word ARMY was stencilled in bold white capitals beside the blue, white and red ringed symbol on the fuselage. At the tail of the chopper Reynolds had been even craftier. Smaller capitals on a red background said DANGER, and a curved white arrow pointed to the rotor blade at the back.

'What think you then?' he asked, looking from Blake to the 'plane and back again. 'She should fool a few screws and jumbos.'

'Very realistic,' Blake agreed. 'Providing they don't look at *us* too closely.'

'No problem there, old thing. I'll be muffled up in m'flying togs, and you can don those.'

He pointed with the brush to an officer's peaked cap and khaki battledress lying on a wooden workbench. Blake walked over and put them on. The jacket was no worse a fit than the one he'd worn in Manston, and the cap snugly gripped his head. The three pips on each shoulder were made of cloth like the ones he'd boasted in Italy nearly thirty years before. Reynolds grinned at him and said:

'Uncanny what a uniform can do.'

'How did you know my rank?'

'Takes one to know one, old thing. I wasn't always as you see me now. I too commanded loyalty and respect.'

'I'm sorry. I didn't mean to—'

'It doesn't hurt any more.'

He put the paint-pot and brush down, took his fleece-lined flying-jacket and helmet from a peg on the wall. Looked at his gadget-littered watch. It was nearly eleven and they had to spring Monkton at noon. He nodded to Blake to help him and together they moved the chopper out into the open. The sky was dark and bloated with rainclouds.

'Summer storm brewing,' said Reynolds casually.

'Will it affect us?'

'Shouldn't do. It's just a milk run from here to Norfolk. If conditions get too bad we'll come down in a field and wait till they blow themselves out. That's the drawback with these whirlybirds. Everything one learnt in fixed-wing flying has to be thrown out the cockpit. If something goes wrong one can't just open the throttle, pull back the stick, and beseech one's Maker. Most modern farmers can fly these jobs better than I!'

Blake laughed and went back to a workbench to collect the canister he'd be using. He checked and made sure it was in ready working order. He carried it aboard the helicopter as carefully and as lovingly as a skydiver with his parachute. He placed it at his feet and strapped himself securely into the red leather passenger seat.

'Hold on to your stomach!' cried Reynolds seconds later, embracing the controls.

There was an impression of lightness, as if they'd been tossed aloft by a giant hand. For a moment Blake thought the blades were going to scrape against the top of the hangar, snap like those of a penknife. But the craft veered to the side and they rose out of danger. The field dropped beneath them and they moved sideways like a vast aerial crab.

Despite what he'd said, Reynolds flew the plane with a tender expertise that was almost too intimate for Blake to watch. He felt like an interloper whose eyes should be bandaged and ears stopped. His embarrassment showed and was misinterpreted. Reynolds shouted above the engine:

'Stop sweating on the top line. Five years is the most you get for helping a prisoner escape.'

'Is that all?'

'Unless he's a spy. Then you have the Official Secrets Act thrown at you as well.'

Blake silently accepted that small mercy. Nothing more was said until he saw the bleak coast of Norfolk, the North Sea spread out like a mudflat behind it. For the first time since they'd taken off, Reynolds screwed his head round to observe him.

'You all geared up?'

Blake nodded.

'Sure of what you have to do?'

Blake reached for the canister, put it reassuringly between his knees. He was aware of a tingling, a sharp spasm that excited and pleasured his groin. But it wasn't the possibility of succeeding that caused the sensation. It was the fear of being caught.

CHAPTER NINETEEN

Seeing Manston from the air for the first time, he was surprised at how unfamiliar and symmetrical it was. He had sacrificed a year of his life behind its walls and still hadn't realized that the prison was star-shaped. Each self-contained wing grew out of a central circle; with a change of inmates and furnishings it could be a showplace, a stately home visited by those whose actions were their own.

As they closed in on it he saw the wing he had been kept in. Behind it, at the far curve of the circle, was the maximum security block; remote, blank, forbidding. Everything now depended upon himself and the next few minutes. He would either spring Monkton, or the job would go catastrophically wrong and he would join him in a cell with a trick floor that betrayed one's every step and movement.

He consulted his watch for the right, synchronized time. Seconds to noon. According to routine, Monkton would be taking his mid-day exercise on the roof. Although Blake couldn't hear it above the engine noise, he knew that a siren would now be sounding in a long, strident wail. It was the dinner signal for the workmen who were reclaiming the swamps. Peering through the side window, he saw them downing their tools, stretching their shoulders, taking out their meal boxes.

The chopper flitted over them, on towards the cons slouching through their various yards, the screws resting at their vantage points. So far, no one had given the 'plane more than an idle glance. It was time for Blake to undo his seat-belt, open the canister and release what it contained. There was a brass handle at the end of the tin which turned to let out the smoke. He gripped it and began to twist. It didn't budge and they were too close to the prison for anything to go wrong. In another thirty seconds they would overshoot it and their chance would be gone.

He was paralysed and unable to act.

Reynolds leant across him and pulled back the sliding panel of the window. His mouth opened gargoyle-fashion as he screamed advice. Blake couldn't hear what he was saying for the uproar of the engine, the bluster of the wind.

He tried reading Reynolds' lips. '*Turn it the other way*,' he was shouting. He did so and the smoke hissed out like poison gas. He held the canister to the window and the smoke tailed dirtily out behind them. From the ground it must have seemed as if the plane was on fire.

Reynolds sat back, squeezed the controls, and they sank abruptly. It was like being in an out-of-control lift. The inside of Blake's chest spewed into his throat and he had a feeling of hollowness. He looked down again and saw the hunched, reptilian figure of Monkton as he stood transfixed on the roof.

He was inside a wire compound. The sides of the fence were three times his height and turned inwards so that it was impossible to climb up and over them. The screw who was guarding him, legs braced and rigid, gaped upwards. The chopper continued to fall until it was fifty . . . twenty . . . ten yards above their heads.

Blake dropped the empty canister, slid back the side door and grappled with the winch attached to the tail ramp. Five hundred feet of thin nylon rope was wound around it, supporting a worn, leather harness suit. He swung out the crank, started the motor, wrestled with the gear stick. The harness snaked down towards Monkton. Even as it did so Blake realized there was no time for the prisoner to strap himself into it. He stopped the winch too soon, and the harness dangled tantalizingly over Monkton's head. He tried to correct it, but something jammed in the gear-box and he couldn't budge the lever.

'Lower, go lower!' he yelled at Reynolds.

They descended inside the wire, hovered like a butterfly caught in a net. Blake leant out of the window, looked into the distintegrating faces of Monkton and the screw.

'Jump, man!' he shouted. 'Jump and get hold of it!'

Monkton did so – twice. But each time his hands failed to grasp the harness. A third attempt and he had the leather crosspiece anchored round his shoulder. The screw emerged from the block of ice he had been frozen in. He started forward, only to be thrust back by the gale caused by the wind and the insanely whirring rotor blades. The chopper swayed and hovered, swayed and hovered.

'I'm pulling you up!' Blake cried.

He turned and forced the winch into reverse. The rope curled in on itself and, spinning like a hanged man, Monkton was raised slowly from the ground. The screw became desperate and spurted. Blake was surprised at how young he was, with the red raw face of a yokel. He reached Monkton and caught hold of him by the knees. Blake wondered if the rope would hold, but it did and Monkton came so near he could smell his breath. He rose until his hands appeared at the edge of the door. If they had to escape and leave him, Blake was ready to stamp on his fingers.

He took hold of Monkton's free arm and helped him scramble halfway inside with the screw still hanging like a deadweight on his legs. It was then that something else went wrong with the winch. The gear jerked into 'forward' and the rope plied out again.

Monkton gasped and slid from view as if through a trap-door. Blake was aware of shouts down below. People running. The prison alarm going off in an hysterical caco-phony of sound. He glanced out and saw that Monkton was almost back on the roof. The screw had his arms around his waist, and was attempting to tear him from the rope.

Blake looked around for a weapon.

Reynolds handed him a spanner, large with an ugly,

angular head. He took it, leant as far out as he dared, and hit the screw on the side of his square-shaped head. A cut materialized as if it had been painted on and he crumpled silently to the ground. Their eyes met as Blake hit him and a message flashed out: *'I'll know you again – anywhere – you bastard!'*

Blake cursed himself for not having smothered-up. His beard, red and straggly, was a dead giveaway. Then it was too late for regrets. The chopper rose as if by suction and the whole chaotic scene was played out in miniature beneath him. The prison and swamps drifted away as Reynolds sent the 'plane scudding low out to sea.

Blake stooped and struggled with the winch. It was no good. The mechanism was stuck, jammed. Monkton would have to stay where he was until the wind plucked him from the harness, committed him to the sea. Blake knew there was only one thing to do: he must pull the man up.

He was in a muck sweat as Reynolds turned the 'plane, and batted inland. They were out of sight of Manston now. The chase, if there was one, would take the pursuing craft towards the continent.

Blake forced himself to look over the side. Monkton was still there twirling lazily on the end of the rope, his features distorted as if he was already drowning. Blake stood, took the nylon rope between his hands and tested the weight. It wasn't much – Monkton was a small, ill-built man – but dragging him in would be beyond most people's power.

He flexed his arm and shoulder muscles. Tried to loop the rope around his wrist; failed, but pulled anyway. The first tug brought Monkton slightly closer to him. He had six inches of loose to play with and let it slip from his grasp onto the floor of the 'plane. He put his foot on it and heaved again. This time it was easier. He jammed his elbow into the rope and used it as an improvised pulley. Another long haul and Monkton's face again came level with the door. He had turned purple and a series of beaded veins marked his forehead.

Blake dragged him up for what he prayed was the last time – noticed the blood that was falling like red rain on Monkton's nose, cheeks, the lids of his half-closed eyes.

The blood was Blake's own and came from the yawning cuts on his hands. Every wound he'd received in the dismantling shop had been sliced open. The blood splattered out. It came in blobs and then in a narrow jet as a fresh cut stung his wrist.

Monkton was unconscious as Blake grabbed him by the armpits and hauled him inside. The door closed and the wind battered furiously against the glass like someone locked out of his own house. Blake squatted and looked at Monkton – at the limp beaten body that bore his name.

I hope all this will be worth it, he thought. I damn well hope it'll be worth it.

CHAPTER TWENTY

The news of Monkton's escape broke midway through the afternoon. It dominated the front pages of both the evening newspapers which Blake scanned on the drive back to Brackley, and he guessed that the television news would be mostly given over to it. He was amused by the indignation and hysteria, the speculation as to Monkton's present whereabouts. Let them search all they liked. Only a fluke would lead them to the slant-ceilinged attic in the Tudor Court. A small, stuffy, priest's-hole of a room hidden behind a steel door marked FIRE EXIT – FOR EMERGENCY USE ONLY. Only a fluke would identify his car as the one which had transported Monkton from Brett Hill to London – the body covered by a raincoat, and then dressed in it as the Yorkshireman gradually regained his senses.

The other thing that pleased him was the fact that the screw he'd hit was out and likely to remain so. There was talk of concussion, brain damage, the chance of him not being able to function normally again.

Blake felt as he had done during the war, when he'd killed a Jerry, or one of his own men had been shot. It was all in the rules of the game. Screws and policemen volunteered for the work they did, and were paid accordingly. If one of them got killed in the process it was part of the old axiom: them or us. He was sorry for the injured man, but suffered from no sense of guilt.

His elation and wellbeing beamed from him. When he got home Karen regarded him as if he'd acquired something (a wig, new teeth) which hadn't been there earlier, and which she didn't entirely approve of.

'You're looking very chipper,' she remarked as she prepared to collect the boys from school.

Blake grinned at her.

'I made quite a haul today.'

'I'm glad you're rehabilitating so well.'

'Didn't you expect me to?'

She turned and made-up her lips in the convex mirror above the fireplace.

'To be honest, darling, I was getting a little dubious.'

'Losing faith in me.'

'Not exactly.'

'Because you've none left to lose?'

She completed the final dab of beauty paint and pirouetted round to him, demanding acclaim. She looked very vital and sexy, he wanted to have her on the carpet.

'Fret not,' she said sweetly. 'Constant Karen – that's me!'

She sidestepped him before he could encircle her waist, jam his genitals against hers. She scrabbled in her purse for her own set of car keys and swayed from the room like a model in a fashion show. She lingered at the door and said as though it had just occurred to her:

'Incidentally, have you heard the latest?'

'The latest what?'

'Prison intelligence. Your pal Monkton has escaped from the hoosegow. He's been bounced or whatever they call it.'

'Sprung.'

'They interrupted women's television to announce it. I thought you'd like to know.'

He waited until she'd left, then went up to the bathroom and washed his hands (which he'd kept hidden from her) under the cold-water tap. The wounds were not as conspicuous as he'd feared. With the blood sponged from them they looked little worse than they had done. Blue and knotted, like tarred-over tramlines.

Satisfied with his repair work, he hurried downstairs to activate the next stage of the plan, the one that would see him in Johannesburg before the month was out. To his annoyance, he found he'd forgotten the number of White

Star, and had to look it up in the book. The girl who answered said her piece automatically.

'White Star Insurance Company. Good afternoon.'

'I'd like to speak to Mr Whitfield.'

'Mr Roy Whitfield?'

'That's him.'

'Who shall I say is calling?'

'Just tell him an old friend and colleague.'

'Putting you through now, sir.'

Someone, thought Blake coldly, is in for a jolt.

CHAPTER TWENTY-ONE

He arranged to meet Whitfield the following lunchtime in a restaurant – El Maghreg – situated on the fringe of the City. He had never been to the place before, and knew little about it except that it was Moroccan, that it featured belly dancers before, with and after the meal, and that it was on the itinerary of most tourists visiting London. They were unlikely to run into anyone from White Star there (too expensive for the workers, too risqué for the bosses); even if they did they were just a couple of old pals out for a boozy and bosomy meal.

He got there fifteen minutes before the stipulated time of one o'clock, and made for the long horseshoe-shaped bar which faced the restaurant proper and the raised cabaret floor beyond. The only illumination came from the red and green lanterns mounted on the tables and protruding at absurd angles from the walls. Behind the bar was a diamond-patterned mirror. He sat staring into it as he sipped his drink, something sour and glutinous called, according to the cocktail list, a Kasbah Kiss.

The establishment proved as popular as the advertisements for it claimed. Americans and foreign visitors arrived at five-minute intervals. They exploded in groups of a dozen or more, were led to tables which comfortably held six, and proceeded to make as much racket as a crowd at a circus.

He was on his second cocktail when Whitfield entered. The blond man paused by the beaded, screen door, peered uncertainly at the tables and stage now lit from underneath by a series of coloured lights, one to each square. Blake waved to him and he came over wiping his neck with a foulard handkerchief. He had on a pearl-grey suit with broad pink stripes, and a zigzagging regimental tie which Blake doubted he was entitled to. He took the circular stool next to Blake, and gazed curiously at the drink.

'What's that you're imbibing?'

'A local brew.'

'I'll have a beer. Danish by choice.'

The barman dressed in a puffed-sleeved shirt, Ali Baba trousers and fez poured him a lager with an unasked-for dash of lime. Whitfield gulped it noisily, spilt some on his mauve silk shirt, dried his chin with his hand.

'Well, Phil,' he said in a boisterous, officers' mess voice. 'Long time no chinwag.'

'It *has* been quite a while, Roy.'

'How are you keeping?'

'Out of prison, mostly.'

Whitfield flushed as much as his broken veins allowed.

'Bad business that all round. They never should have prosecuted.'

'What do you think they should have done? Turned a liberally blind eye?'

'Given you the benefit of another chance. Mean to say, everyone has their little fiddle.'

'Present company included.'

'Look here, old man, I had the decency to come along and see you. Under no obligation, you know. Could easily have been bloody minded and declined.'

'Declined?' Blake echoed. 'You wouldn't dare.'

'Just doing the decent thing.'

'You wouldn't know the decent thing if it came up and kicked you in the pills.'

For a moment Blake thought he'd pushed him too hard and too soon. Whitfield blew out his cheeks, stood up, prepared to make an outraged exit. Blake was just about to anchor him by the wrist, when there was a drum-roll, a reverberation of cymbals, and two near-naked girls contorted their way onto the stage. The manager appeared as if through a trapdoor, stood in front of Whitfield with his arms outspread.

'You can't leave now, sir. Not till you've seen Lallé and Hayali.'

'The belly dancers,' Blake explained, nodding to the stage. 'You'll cause an international incident if you walk out now.'

Whitfield sat unwillingly down again, ordered another lager, did not get a drink in for Blake. They watched the dancers go into a bump-and-grind routine which Blake found neither comic nor sexy. It pleased the diners, however, and he only hoped it didn't give them indigestion afterwards.

'All right, Blake,' said Whitfield stiffly. 'I'll give you five minutes in which to say your piece.'

'Cards on the table and all that.'

'If it's money you're after, the answer is decisively "no".'

'Information is all I want.'

'Info. What sort?'

'Goods in transit.'

'And if I choose to withhold it?'

Blake took a coin from his pocket, spun it idly on the bar. 'Then I shall be obliged to make a 'phone call to White Star. A conscience call.'

'You've got nothing on me, old man.'

'Evidentially, I've less on you than those girls are wearing. But I know what to tell, and who to tell.'

'There's such a thing as the law of slander, Blake. Don't you forget that.'

'Only a guilty man would meet one threat with another one.'

'If this is blackmail—'

'What else?'

It was hot where they were sitting, but not hot enough to account for the sweat which gushed out of Whitfield's pores, ran like glycerine down his cheeks.

'Let me spell it out for you,' said Blake. 'Then you can leave unhandcuffed.'

'For Christ's sake be discreet!'

Blake twisted round on the stool, watched the dancers with the required degree of lechery. Whitfield was perspiring so much he didn't have to act.

'As you well know,' Blake murmured, 'four times a year a consignment of South African diamonds is flown to

London to be sighted at De Beers. Most of the stones are already shaped, and the sights are attended by dealers from all over the world. They also buy the parcels of rough, and take them back to their respective countries to be cut into irregular and classical forms.

'The summer consignment, which is due at any time now, is the year's most valuable haul. Rich in the four c's – carat weight, colour, clarity and cut. It will mostly end up in New York, at the House of Diamonds. Are you with me?'

'Ahead of you, old man.'

'Fine. Then you'll know what I'm going to ask next.'

'The date of the flight. The airline. The flight number.'

'Three out of three.'

'If I do divulge these, will it be the end of our ... association?'

'Pos-i-tively.'

'No more menacing 'phone calls?'

'I asked you out for a drink, Roy; remember?'

Whitfield sighed and rubbed his forehead as if it was paining him. The dancers were approaching the climax of their act. They jiggled to the rim of the stage, worked their pelvises in a way women seldom do in bed. The tourists, male and female, began shouting encouragement; whistling, stamping, clapping their hands above their heads.

'The consignment you're interested in leaves Jo'burg a week on Thursday.'

'Jan Smuts airport?'

'It'll be put on a Boeing 747 and flown out here in the morning. It's the only CAC flight that day.'

'CAC?'

'Cape Airways Corporation.'

'Don't they use BOAC or South African Airways any more?'

'Alternatively. This is a new outfit which has recently set up in opposition. A similar service, but cheaper allround fares.'

'Including cargo rates?'

'Especially those. That's how they're scoring over their rivals. It'll be the second diamond freight they've carried for us.'

'The same means of delivery.'

'Registered mailbags.'

'With the Universal Postal Union label.'
'They'll never learn.'
Blake rose, left the bill for Whitfield to pay.
'Perhaps they will this time. Old man.'

CHAPTER TWENTY-TWO

It took an hour for the telephone call to come through. Whitfield spent the time patrolling his office, going to the lavatory, sending his secretary out on improvised errands. Despite the talcs and deodorants he used, a smell came from him – high and sour, that of an animal trapped in a cave. He wiped his armpits with a handkerchief, was alone when the tomato-red instrument on his desk bleeped demandingly at him. He raised the receiver, glad he had not taken his brandy flask from the middle drawer of the filing-cabinet. His voice needed to be firm, purposeful, in charge. A few seconds of protocol and he made contact.

'Yes?'

'It's Whitfield here. Roy Whitfield.'

'So?'

'It's about Blake.'

'You'll have to speak-up,' said the man with the hearing-aid. 'I'm not getting you.'

Whitfield cupped his hand over his lips, shouted into the mouthpiece.

'I have news of Philip Blake.'

'Couldn't you have used the telex?'

'It's confidential.'

'Go on.'

'He's been in touch with me. I had drinks with him this lunchtime.'

'And?'

'He's planning something. Some kind of revenge.'

'Revenge?'

'Against the company.'

Pause.

'Tell me about it.'

Whitfield did so – giving an account in which he wasn't blackmailed, merely approached and propositioned.

'Not that he learned anything from me. I just confirmed what he already knew.' There was a pithy silence as he ended his report. His throat ached and his tie seemed to be tightening.

'Is that all?'

'Everything, sir. I can have him picked-up if you—'

'Forget it.'

'But if he *does* carry out—'

Let him, thought the man with the hearing-aid as he dismissed Whitfield and told him to wait instructions.

Why should I deny him more rope?

CHAPTER TWENTY-THREE

For Blake the next few days passed as slowly and monotonously as they had done in Manston. With no work to occupy him he travelled up to the West End each day and spent the time in pubs, bars, restaurants and drinking clubs. He knew drink and could handle it as an adversary of his own weight and size. But pint by pint, measure by measure, he discovered he was losing the contest. Not that he felt in any danger of final defeat. But he realized it would be a points decision, a toss-up, a close thing.

Take the morning he met Bart. A noon-time appointment in the palm-bedecked bar of the Tudor Court. He arrived early and had downed three large brandies by the time Bart waddled self-importantly into the room. The accountant ordered a mint julep and brought it over to the table which cramped Blake at the knees. Bart watched him start on his fourth double Hine and shook his head worriedly.

'You want to take it easy on that stuff, Phil. You can't depend on it when it comes to the crunch.'

'How else am I to kill time? I've seen four films so far this week. Each one a parody of the one before.'

'Can't you stay at home?'

'My wife considers me legitimately employed. Earning money – not boozing it away.'

'Perhaps these will restore your sobriety.'

Bart slid his hand into his inside breast pocket and took

out two slim manilla folders. He skated them across the glass table-top where they lay before Blake like poker cards waiting to be turned. He picked up the longer of the two, opened it as though drawing to a royal flush. An airline ticket (CAC) and some illustrated leaflets about South Africa. The ticket, in pastel blue and white, particularly intrigued him. It was first class, round-trip, and cost £545·50.

He whistled appreciatively.

'Ritzy!'

'Only way to do it. You and Clancy will be travelling together as men of independence and means.'

'And how are you getting to Jo'burg?'

'Trek Airways. It's not scheduled with the International Air Transport Association, and is roughly a third of the cost.'

'Why don't we all go that way?'

'The first reason I've already given to you.'

'And the second?'

'You'll be on a pre-selected 747 activating phase two.'

'The air stewardesses.'

'Les girls.'

Blake hesitated, knotted his hands, and said uncertainly: 'I'm worried about them, Bart. I'm no womaniser. Suppose they don't take a shine to me. Or to Clancy?'

'Fret not. They already have.'

'But how—'

'Why else do you think Clancy's aboard? For the past week he's been sniffing around them like an African wild dog. Between flights they frequent a club in Springbok Valley, or Earl's Court as it's also known. Lover-boy has got them going like bitches on heat. He's already mounted his. Your's has been told all about you, even shown your picture. I promise you, she's more than interested; she's intrigued. Seems she has a father fixation, prefers older men providing they're not prolapsed.'

'So there's no problem.'

'Nor should be.'

Blake relaxed his hands, put the travel folder in his wallet.

'Incidentally,' he said, 'who bought these? Or were they "acquired"?'

'We dipped into the monk's treasure trove.'

'Is he still?' He nodded towards the ceiling.

'We moved him yesterday to the Midlands. Where his bank is.'

'His bank!'

'Under another name he has a very respectable and healthy account with a bank in Wolverhampton.'

'So crime *does* pay!'

'Spasmodically.'

'When do Clancy and I take off, then?'

'Heathrow, tomorrow at 8 a.m. You'll be in Jo'burg for supper.'

'Good job my passport's in order.'

'Wouldn't matter if it wasn't.'

'It wouldn't?'

'Take a shufty in the other envelope.'

Blake did so and found a passport – not too new, not too battered – in the name of Paul Bennett. His profession was 'Writer', covering a multitude of eccentric activities and behaviour. There was a picture of Blake complete with incipient beard, and the descriptions had been correctly filled in.

'How much did this set Monkton back?' he asked.

'A twoer.'

'Then he's been had.'

'How?'

'The "artist" omitted the section about hair, colour of.'

'At least give *me* credit for knowing what I'm doing. The passport office no longer bothers with such a variable element.'

'It doesn't?'

'We're living in an age of weaves, wigs and washes.'

'If I wore one, I'd take off my hairpiece to you.'

'Do me another favour instead.'

'Name it.'

'Splice your brandy with soda. You're getting that swimmy look about the face. As if you're going under for the third time.'

'You could save me from anything, Bart.'

'Except yourself.'

He told Karen that night about his leaving, and expected

there to be a token demonstration of regret. A few tears, real or crocodile; some sentiments of envy and wifely despair. She was preparing dinner in the steel womb of the kitchen when he broke the news, and her reaction could not have been more impassive. It was only when he went into details about the trip (as a 'writer' his imagination had been recharged) that she betrayed any misgivings.

'This job of yours, Phil,' she said tightly. 'You're quite sure you've told me everything about it? There's nothing you're concealing or keeping back?'

He helped himself to a handful of raw peas.

'Such as?'

'I don't know exactly. It all seems so . . . convenient.'

'Wasn't I due for a break?'

'– Yes.'

'But?'

'It just doesn't feel right.'

'In that case refuse the money I'll be making.'

'It's not ethics that's bothering me. I'm sure it's all very legal and aboveboard.'

'As much as anything is nowadays.'

'I suppose I'm just being feminine and boringly intuitive.'

'Or plain superstitious.'

'Whatever it is, darling, I want you to be careful. Very careful.'

'You haven't been having prophetic dreams, have you? Or seeing doom in the tealeaves?'

'I seldom remember dreams, and we use tea-bags.'

'Then it's just an irrational premonition.'

'If you like.'

'I remember the last time you had one. Shortly before my "discovery and arrest". . . . I didn't listen to you then, either.'

'And look what happened.'

To the side of them, the frying-pan suddenly spat. A slug of oil landed on the terracotta tiles, lay there making insect-like noises. He strode over and squashed it underfoot.

'If anything does go wrong,' he said deliberately, 'I promise you one thing.'

'What's that?'

'I'll give you grounds for divorce.'

'If that's how *you* want it.'

'And the boys? What would become of the boys?'

'I'd take them with me to Cape Town.'

'Straight into daddy's ever-open arms.'

She looked at him sideways; reproachfully; like a bad conscience.

'Until then, I'll stay in yours.'

PHASE THREE

CHAPTER TWENTY-FOUR

He used the Renault to drive to Heathrow, left it in the car-park there awaiting his return. He'd arranged to meet Clancy by the bookstall in the main building and walked through the anonymous bustle as buoyant and uncaring as a youngster on his first trip abroad. He spotted Clancy eyeing a rack of sex magazines. A healthy young animal in t-shirt, sky-blue nylon windcheater and fitted jeans, a 'Rolieflex' slung from his neck like a third eye. They greeted each other civilly but without real warmth. Underwent some brief but irritating passport formalities and joined the rest of the passengers for Johannesburg at gate number nine.

Their fellow-travellers, thought Blake, were a characterless, stereotyped lot. He could see them on any West End street, suburban bus, or commuter train. He dismissed them as harmless and concentrated on the two stewardesses posed in lime-green uniforms, exchanging knowing jokes and giggles with the CAC ground ambassador. They represented the first stage of the three million pound coup. If they failed with them then the whole job was in jeopardy. He glanced at Clancy, who gave him a confident wink.

'The redhead's mine,' he muttered. 'That leaves the blonde mystery for you.'

Re-examining the girls, Blake saw the Cockney had made the obvious but right choice. The taller, plumper and more flamboyant of the two, the redhead, was lounging one knee over the other, hand on fleshy hip. Her hair was a bubble bath of strawberry curls, her lips were bee stung, her breasts strained teasingly against the button-up tunic she wore over her hot pants. She might have been fashioned for Clancy's virile attentions.

Her blonde companion, slim and flat as a boy, appeared more aloof, frigid, difficult to fool. Her long, champagne-coloured hair was parted in the centre, and her pale face peered delicately through the middle of it. She saw Blake staring at her and her eyes glazed protectively, as if screens had dropped over them. He turned his head and inspected the 747, its bull's-eye nose raised high above the foot of the pier, a service tanker attached to its belly like a piglet suckling a sow.

He was happy to be ignored for the moment, pleased that she was tactful and discreet. It wasn't until they had trudged down the pier, and boarded the plane, that he realized Clancy and he were almost the only first-class passengers. They sat in the foremost cabin, between the bulbous flight deck and the underslung podded jets which seemed to be on stalks. Their over-stuffed tangerine seats distinguished them from the people in tourist. Put them at one with the bespectacled man taking documents from a briefcase, the elderly woman – in suede catsuit and furs – who was cramming her mouth with travel sickness pills.

When the stewardess came to check the names with her seat chart it was the redhead who entered the cabin. She went to the businessman first, cajoled the anxiety from his face, showed him how to use the fingertip selection of the twelve-channel music and movie soundtrack. While she did this Clancy, who was seated on the aisle, unslung his camera and parked it into the overhead compartment. He gave Blake another wink and leant back so that his chest knotted beneath his shirt. A moment later the redhead was beside him, her mouth unzipped in a professional smile.

'Excuse me, sir,' she said correctly, as if they had never met before. 'But do you mind if I close the compartment?'

Clancy squeezed up his eyes and glowered at her.

''S'matter'fact I do.'

'It's a company regulation, sir.'

'So what happens to me gear?'

'You may leave it in there until after take-off.'

'I'll have it on me knee.'

'Certainly, sir.'

She stretched on tiptoe and leaned across him to reach the compartment. Blake smelt her perfume, thick and candid, blinked as her tunic rose to reveal an inch of spongy skin. Her navel was directly above Clancy's mouth, his breath blew into it like wind into a cave. She took the camera, lifted it carefully down, did no more than shudder as he flicked out his tongue, pressed it against her belly button.

'Here we are, sir. Now; if I could have your name and profession?'

Clancy gave his new name of 'Carter', adding that he was a photographer, 'And I don't mean no smudge merchant, neither.' The stewardess noted this and looked enquiringly at Blake.

'Bennett,' he said. 'B-e-n-n-e-t-t. I'm a writer. Or didn't you know?'

'Just for the record, sir.'

She made another squiggle on her pad.

'A writer and photographer. Quite the Pulitzer team.'

'That's us,' Blake nodded. 'We're doing a feature on the rand for one of the colour supplements.'

'How fascinating.'

'That depends,' put in Clancy, 'on the co-operation we get. Makin' friends with the populace like.'

'I'm sure you'll have no difficulty there, sir.'

'You can put us on to some friendly people?'

'I can only speak for myself, sir.'

'So speak.'

'I'll attend to your wants later, sir.'

'All of 'em?'

'All that I can.'

She bowed her head and moved across to the woman who was opening her second tube of Kwells.

'Home in one again,' said Clancy smugly. 'Now let's see you score.'

Despite his eagerness, it wasn't until after lunch – breaded veal, french fries, and orange shine, served in plastic containers in his lap – that Blake got within speaking distance of the blonde senior stewardess. Her name, she announced blandly over the intercom, was Miss Van Heerden. She wished everyone a pleasant flight, said that a film, *The Sound of Music*, would be shown, and that drinks would be served in the upstairs first-class lounge.

'My colleague, Miss Bierman, and I will be in attendance in the bar.' She concluded, 'I must again apologize for the lack of service on today's flight. But due to a restricted staff strike we can only muster a skeleton crew.'

Blake stood up, yawned, gazed through the window at the bare blue vault of the sky. He'd heard of people feeling spiritually elated and near to God when thirty-thousand feet above the hidden earth. But it didn't affect him that way. He was bored, restless, in need of a drink. He flipped his hand at Clancy and mounted the short spiral staircase to the upstairs lounge, arc-shaped with scarlet and mustard yellow furnishings. The room was empty save for the blonde, Miss Van Heerden, who was leaning with an elbow on the bar. She had a lilac silk scarf around her neck, and she fiddled with the ends of it as he padded along the fitted carpet towards her. He stopped at the bar and gave her time to adjust her smile.

'Hello,' he said brightly. 'Thought I'd take you up on that drink.'

'The movie doesn't appeal to you, sir?'

'The orange shine was sweetness enough.'

'What would you prefer, sir?'

'I'd prefer me a brandy.'

'French or South African, sir?'

'I'm hoping to sample the wines of the country.'

'Then I'd recommend the Oude Meester, sir.'

'And I'll accept it – on one condition.'

'Sir?'

'That you stop calling me sir.'

'It's company policy, sir.'

'It's also Army policy – and I was demobbed before you were born.'

She smiled vaguely and poured him a solid measure of brandy. He took the tumbler from her, refused ginger ale or soda, and swallowed deeply. A bracing finger of warmth poked his throat.

'Is this your first visit to South Africa, sir?' she asked as he held out the glass for a refill.

'The first of many, I hope.'

'Miss Bierman tells me you're a writer.'

'Journalist.'

'You're not published in book form?'

'Articles, articles, articles.'

'That's a good way to start – serious writing, I mean.'

'You're very knowledgeable.'

'I majored in English at Witwatersrand University. Much good that it did me.'

'Why, don't you like being a stewardess?'

'It's a living – while it lasts.'

'A short life but a well-travelled one.'

'They retire us at thirty-two.'

'And take back the oyster.'

'Oyster?'

'You know, the world.'

'That's what Miss Bierman says. It's on loan with a short string attached.'

'Sensible girl, your friend. By the way, where is she right now?'

'In the cattle car.'

'Pardon?'

'The tourist section, where the free booze is limited to two drinks a thirsty head.'

'I feel privileged.'

'You're paying for it.'

He raised his glass to her.

'Here's to my trip. May it be a companionable one.'

She hesitated for a second, as if coming to a decision. Then murmured:

'What a shame your wife can't be with you.'

He had the tumbler to his mouth before the significance of her words hit him. For a moment he thought Clancy had told her his name was really Blake, and that he was married to the former Karen Petersen. Then he realized how ridiculous that was, and lowered the glass.

'Who said I was married?' he demanded.

She smiled artfully.

'One can usually tell, sir.'

'How can one usually tell?'

'The way you entered the bar just now, for instance. All male bravado and bonhomie. Bachelors never approach a stew like that. They are much more devious.'

'Is that all?'

'There was your address.'

'My address!' He remembered putting a phoney address label on his suitcase – a fictitious street in one of the outer suburbs.

'Only married men live in Pinner and such places,' she said, twirling the bottom of her scarf.

'They do?'

'Bachelors have "chic little central apartments". Unless they're fixated and live with their mothers.'

'At least I'm not that.'

'But you *are* married, sir?'

'Divorced.'

'So that accounts for the white finger.'

'The what?'

'The white skin where your wedding ring used to be. Some men take it off before boarding the plane.'

He extended his left hand. She was right; there was a white band there, like grass that had been covered by a piece of wood all winter. The ring Karen gave him when they were married had been removed after his accident in the dismantling shop. He hadn't replaced it as his finger was still tender at the joint.

'*That*!' he exclaimed. 'I didn't even know it was there.'

'Most men would. And they'd have done something about it.'

'Such as?'

'Covered it with flesh-coloured make-up.'

'You have got the masculine sex sized up.'

'Only when I'm interested – sir.'

'Then you can show your interest by having a drink with me.'

'It's against company policy, sir. "Conduct unbecoming a stewardess".'

'Screw company policy.'

'Yes, sir.'

CHAPTER TWENTY-FIVE

'Time to wake up, sir,' said Miss Van Heerden in his ear. 'We are due in Johannesburg in five minutes.'

Blake opened his eyes and saw her narrow waxen face, her hair falling forward in two platinum strands. The last thing he remembered was of her helping him from the bar and back to his seat; a foolish attention-focusing struggle in the lobby at the bottom of the stairs; the affronted comments of the airsick lady who had brandished her brown paper bag at him.

'What happened?' he asked dully.

'It must have been the Oude Meester, sir. It's heady stuff when you're not used to it.'

'I can hold my brandy.'

'And there was a slight case of cat.'

'Who?'

'Clear air turbulence. You were warned about it during oxygen mask drill.'

He sat up and looked around for Clancy. The Cockney's seat was vacant except for his trim CAC bag.

'Your friend will be back in a moment,' she said. 'He and Miss Bierman are getting re-acquainted.'

'So the natives *are* friendly.'

'Of course, sir. It's—'

'Don't tell me,' he groaned. 'It's company policy.'

She reissued her smile and crossed to awaken the businessman, whose briefcase was cradled on his knees like a pampered pet. Still feeling weak and groggy (he must have sunk eight or nine brandies), Blake looked down on what seemed to be an illuminated gridiron. The sky over Johannesburg was purple streaked with pink, the lights from the skyscraper blocks blinked and glittered like diamonds set in concrete slabs. A tall slender tower (the Albert Hertzog he learned later) pricked the undersides of the violet clouds. He could see the scarlet ribbons of traffic as the 747 tilted and circled the city. There was an announcement apologizing for the landing delay and Clancy swaggered back, his crotch as taut and swollen as a ballet dancer's.

'Stage two successfully completed,' he said as he rejoined Blake.

'When are you seeing her next?'

'Tomorrow night. There's a party on and I'm invited.'

'Great.'

'How did you make out?'

'I'm not sure yet.'

'She's playing hard to get?'

'To grips with.'

He didn't obtain the answer until they landed at Jan Smuts Airport, and were filing out to leave the 'plane. The two stewardesses stood at the exit, demonstrating their teeth and chanting: 'A pleasant stay in the City of Gold'. As Blake passed the blonde she shook hands with him and pressed a slip of pasteboard into his palm. He examined it on the bus which took him and Clancy along the freeway and into the city centre. Miss Denise Van Heerden, a Hillbrow address that meant nothing to him, and an all-digit telephone number.

They left the bus at the airways terminal off Wolmarans Street, and took a cab to their hotel, the Tollman Towers. It was one of the best and most expensive in Johannesburg, and they'd been booked in there by Bart as part of their international jet-set image. A light rain was falling as they got out and entered the marble lobby. Ahead of them a party of clamorous Australians just returned from some cabaret or nightclub made an incident out of getting their room keys. At last they stomped away, lashing each other with transparent raincoats.

After Blake's ordeal, the reception clerk was still crisp and efficient. It was only when Blake asked for 'Mr Bainbridge' that his mask finally cracked.

'Is he expecting you, sir?' he asked apprehensively.

'Very much so.'

'I'll check to see if he can receive visitors.'

'Is something wrong with him?'

'Mr Bainbridge has been . . . unwell, sir.'

'Unwell?'

'He suffered a . . . slight seizure, sir.'

'When?'

'Yesterday morning.'

Beside him, Clancy stiffened and sucked in his breath.

'How slight?'

'A doctor was called, sir. I believe that Mr Bainbridge is holding his own.'

They were afraid to look at each other while the clerk rang through on an internal telephone. He came back relieved, as though death was not about to embarrass the management.

'I have spoken with your friend and he's asked you to go straight up. Apparently he is feeling much stronger.'

A porter showed them into the elevator which shot them, without sense of speed or motion, to the twenty-third floor.

The suite Bart occupied was done out in 'typico' Spanish style. They found him sitting in a high-backed chair in the drawing-room – his body shrunken, his face the colour of flax. Blake tipped the porter, waited until he had noiselessly withdrawn. For a moment the three men regarded each other like strangers. Then Bart said weakly:

'Sorry to lumber you like this. The quack said I shouldn't be left alone.'

'He's the expert,' Blake muttered.

'A nurse was out of the question, and—'

'Don't labour it.'

He waved his hands in apology.

'I always was a jinx.'

'You should have stayed in London. Clancy and I can handle this on our own.'

'Very likely, Phil. But after Manston I needed the experience. To know I hadn't lost my touch.'

Blake spotted a bar set into the wall flanked by fancy ironwork, lanterns and scrolls. He went over to it and poured himself a drink, tasted it without knowing what it was.

'So what gives now?' demanded Clancy. 'Do we scrub the whole deal?'

Bart looked sharply at him.

'No cause for extremes, Mike. We go ahead as planned.'

'With a flaming invalid in tow!'

'I am not *tot*ally immobile. I have enough drugs to get me through the job and home again.'

'And how soon will that be?' asked Blake.

He squirmed and tugged his dressing-gown closer around him.

'Three days at the most.'

'You're sure of that?'

'Despite my . . . indisposition, I have not been exactly idle. The diamonds will be flown into London on Friday, on the same plane you arrived in. There should be ample time to lift the tomfoolery before you reach Heathrow. As long as you complete *your* groundwork.'

'We have almost,' Blake said, and told him of their progress with the stewardesses.

Bart nodded approvingly.

'Remember they can be useful to us before the return

flight. Any inside information you can pick up promotes the success of our operation.'

They spent the next half-hour going over the plan until they could have recited it backwards, sideways, in code if necessary. It was past midnight when the conference ended and Blake helped Bart to the couch on which he preferred to sleep.

'I'm unable to turn in this, and it lessens the strain,' he explained. The others had twin beds in the next room, and Blake fell asleep listening to the whisper of rain on the window, the wind that washed it gently against the building.

The last word he said to himself was:

'Jinx'.

CHAPTER TWENTY-SIX

The doctor who came to see Bart in the morning, a diminutive blue-chinned Afrikaans called Pretorius, sent Clancy and Blake from the drawing-room while he made his examination. They stood on the terrace of their suite gazing like visiting gods on the early-morning turmoil of Johannesburg. The rows of skyscrapers, stuck like giant pegs in the ground with newer, uncompleted pegs rising beside them gave a weird sense of impermanence. The straight concrete canyons of the streets also seemed too arbitrary to last, and Blake unexpectedly felt nostalgic for the clustered muddle of London and its ravelled, interlinking villages. A greasy film of smog pressed down on the scene, and past it he discerned the horizon of sallow mine dumps with dust smoking from them.

He was still feeling the city's pulse when Dr Pretorius came out on the balcony, carrying a black bag that seemed too large and heavy for him.

'Impressive, is it not?' he said, nodding to the view. 'Providing you like the world of tomorrow today.'

'It is somewhat futuristic,' Blake agreed.

'Cape Town. Now, there's a darling, a woman you can caress and hold. Jo'burg is her idiot sister.'

'But still exciting.'

'All you rednecks say that at first.'

'Rednecks?'

'Newcomers – the sun brands you for what you are.'

'We won't be here long enough for that,' rasped Clancy. 'A quick in and out.'

The doctor looked at him distastefully.

'Just as well for your friend's sake.'

'How ill is he?' asked Blake.

'He'll live as long as he chooses to.'

'Meaning?'

'In a wheelchair, with skilled attention, he could possibly see the century out.'

'And otherwise?'

'Any undue activity, any tension or upset, and you'll be flying him home in a box.'

'Thanks for being honest.'

'You can thank me best,' he said pointedly, 'by settling my account now.'

Later, when the doctor had taken his fee and gone, Blake told Bart that from then on he was a sleeping partner in the firm. He could advise, direct and organize; anything more strenuous than that was out. The sick man accepted the fact stoically. 'The quack says I'll survive till this evening, so go and amuse yourselves,' he bid. 'The day after tomorrow we'll set the machine in motion.'

It was easily said, but the prospect of hours of sightseeing and rubbernecking depressed Blake. Apart from the job, he and Clancy had nothing in common. So out of professional duty, he took Miss Van Heerden's card from his wallet and went down to ring her from the lobby.

Downstairs, the activity cheered him. A group of Bantus, huddled beneath striped umbrellas, gaped in through the glass doors – the men in English-type suits that were ten years out of fashion, the women in skirts and head-scarves of bold primary colours. It took a long time for the Hillbrow number to answer, and he pictured the stewardess cursing the caller for interrupting her lie-in; or, worse, unwrapping herself from the embrace of some lusty young stud, talking to him while her lover kissed every part of her body but her mouth. Her voice, when it came, was suspiciously hushed.

'Hello,' he saluted. 'This is your white-fingered friend.'

'Who?'

'I took on a bottle of Oude Meester last night, and lost.'
'Mr Barnet!'
'Bennett. You gave me your card.'
'Thank you for calling so soon.'
'Is it too early for you?'
'What time is it? I'm wearing a sleeping-mask.'
'Tennish.'
'A.m., or p.m.?'
'The sun is reddening my neck.'
'You *are* learning fast!'
'I was going to ask you out to lunch. Or is dating passengers considered conduct unbecoming?'
'A fringe benefit.'
'Shall we say one o'clock.'
'Where?'
'You name it, I'll be there.'
'The Zoo Lake restaurant is "rather chic".'
'One o'clock, then.'
'Local time.'

She hung up and he strode out into the open prison of the city. Encouraged by his reception, the morning passed more rapidly and agreeably than he'd thought. He window-shopped, sat in the gardens of the old library, wandered downtown and loitered for a while on Diamond Corner. Further on he had coffee at a pavement cafe, his table flanked by tubs of tropical plants. At 12.45 he was swaying in a black Buick cab along Jan Smuts Avenue, *en route* for the zoo.

He got out near the lake, watched a coloured nurse help two small boys feed the birds in the water, and secured a table in the restaurant's outside court. He sat facing the sun, his neck shielded by a vine-laced trellis. He was on his first beer when she rounded the corner and walked daintily towards him. Out of uniform, in a short lemon-coloured dress and matching picture hat, she seemed even smaller and curiously defenceless. He rose to greet her, wondering what her hazel eyes made of him.

'Starting early,' she said as she smoothed her skirt and sat down.

'A bald dog wouldn't miss this hair.'
'Don't you suffer from hangovers?'
'Rarely.'

She tutted playfully.

'That *is* a bad sign. The last passenger who dated me had a head like a rugby ball the next day. He said it felt as if the Springboks were practising with it.'

'You go out with many passengers?'

'In your case I was forewarned. Besides, we're conditioned to be polite. We were taught at training school that everyone is a potential customer. And must always be treated as such.'

'But I've already made my flight.'

'There's the return trip. How do I know you mightn't be all hurt and wounded, and go OLP?'

'Translation, please.'

'Travel as an off-line passenger on BOAC or SAA.'

'And miss stratospheric cocktails with you!'

'I would hate for you to do that.'

He broke off and ordered from the waiter who had followed her to the table. She wanted only a prawn soufflé and peach sherbet, but Blake let himself go on marinated lamb, scalloped potatoes, three kinds of vegetables, with soup first and a cheese pudding for afters.

'Are you dieting?' he asked, as the soufflé came and she pecked disinterestedly at it.

'All we stews have to. We conform to a listed weight. A pound over it and you're suspended until you've starved it off.'

'You should have no problem.'

'Not yet. But I'd dread to be like Freda – Miss Bierman. She's in the apartment now sweating over a hot exercise-machine.'

'You share a flat with her.'

'In Hillbrow Galleries. It's very chic and self-contained. You can live, shop and sunbathe without leaving the premises.'

'Sounds ideal.'

'Until we're brusquely asked to leave.'

'For why?'

She pushed her plate from her, the edifice of eggs and fish undemolished.

'Most landlords disapprove of stews as tenants. As we're only at home half of the time, they think we form a broken chain of booze and orgies.'

'And do you?'

'Come along tonight and find out.'

So far the meal had gone on conventional man-chats-up-girl lines, and he'd gleaned none of the inside information Bart wanted. He finished the cheese and ordered two glasses of Van der Hum, and a long black cigar. He was about to resume his questioning, but Denise put a finger to her lips.

'Enough about my life and chic times. Tell me about yourself. How your assignment's going, for instance.'

He had forgotten about his supposed article for a colour supplement, and improvised on his instant impressions of Johannesburg.

'That's a journalist's lot for you,' he ended ruefully. 'Three days in a "thrilling city" and you're supposed to describe it as if you were on the voting list.'

'Perhaps your return flight will provide more colourful copy.'

'Short of a hijacking, I doubt it.'

'Hijackers get nowhere fast with us,' she said airily. 'The cockpit door is kept closed and locked at all times – the same as the luggage bays. Every stew carries the keys under her jacket, and no one is allowed into *that* territory.'

'So much for drama.'

She squinted and looked beyond them to where some swimmers were scampering towards the pool.

'I wouldn't say that.'

'What would you say?'

'Just that we'll be carrying a "very valuable freight" in the first-class cargo bay. I shouldn't even tell you that much. But as you're a top journalist I can always claim you wormed it out of me.'

'We journalists never disclose our sources.'

'Someone could make a grab for the cargo at the other end. It's been tried before. That's what the guard's for.'

He bit into his cigar.

'What guard?'

'The man who'll be sitting with the bulge under his armpit.'

'Bulge?'

'Where his gun is, dumdum. Don't you ever watch gangster films?'

'Only if forced.'

'Over here they're considered an "extremely dangerous influence". Zulus and blacks are forbidden to see them by law.'

She prattled on about security, and he heard her as if she was speaking from down a well. By including Clancy in the caper, Bart had provided for locked doors. But an armed guard was something he hadn't reckoned on. In his present condition, Blake doubted if he could.

CHAPTER TWENTY-SEVEN

As it was a 'strike party' they were going to, Blake convinced Clancy to do the gallant thing and buy two bottles of Cape brandy from a liquor store in Smit Street, which they tracked along that evening on their way to Hillbrow. During an afternoon spent musing over the guard problem, Blake decided to say nothing about it to Bart. He was frightened the news would bring on another heart spasm, and he told Clancy only to stop the Cockney from accusing him later of deceit.

Denise had drawn a lipstick map on the inside of a cigarette packet showing the way to the highrise block in which she and her flat-mate lived. The sun was setting over Johannesburg in a technicolour explosion as the two men reached the district with its profusion of coffee bars, boutiques, discotheques and nightclubs. The streets were awash with casually dressed young people who moved faster and with more purpose than their equivalents in England. Clancy responded to the animation, swaggered like a sailor on shore-leave as they entered the Galleries, took the elevator to the tenth floor.

The door to the girls' apartment was open, and they were drawn inside by the magnet of oriental music, laughter, the determined chatter of people too self-conscious not to speak. A pall of cigarette smoke gave a second ceiling to the living-room, and Blake spotted Denise in a purple and mauve sari talking to a tall square-jawed man with conspicuously white hair. She unlinked hands with him as she saw Blake, glided over on invisible wheels.

'Hi,' she called out gaily. 'Welcome to the stew zoo.'

He stooped and kissed her offered cheek, his lips dry and grating her skin. The man smiled over at them, his teeth like plastic shields.

'Who's the boyfriend?' Blake asked casually.

'Carl. Don't you think he's groovy?'

'If you go for male models.'

'And miaow to you,' she said, leading him towards the drinks table. 'But you're not all that wrong. He's the captain of the 'plane you flew in. And he also does modelling on the side. Y-pants and string vests mostly.'

'How versatile.'

'All we aircrew are. But you haven't experienced that yet, have you?'

'Why else am I here?'

'You tell me.'

They reached the table and Blake placed the brandy among the bottles of wine and spirits; the pyramids of Texans and Lucky Strikes; the foil-wrapped soles, lobsters, steaks and salmon.

'*Not there!*' she protested, moving the brandy to the left of the array. 'That's Freda's stockpile.'

He gazed at the banquet of food and drink.

'Are all these offerings?'

'Mostly. Some of it Freda and I acquired from the galley.'

'Another fringe benefit.'

'What would life be without them?'

'Barren.'

She gave a bright social laugh and steered him into the midst of the guests, most of whom were under thirty and dauntingly beautiful. She introduced him to a cross-section of sharp-faced men – all questions and prepackaged answers; girls who regarded him with pert interest, as if he was fresh from another planet. A further touch of his elbow, and Denise veered away – the perfect hostess, making sure everyone present received their quota of charm, warmth and welcome.

For the next two hours, he was shuttled from group to group, person to person, like a goodwill ambassador from the 'old country'. His secondhand anecdotes about London, Carnaby Street, Soho and Chelsea were practically greeted with applause.

'You know,' said one rouged and bewigged woman,

older and coyer than the rest. 'I could just stand here and listen to your accent all night.'

By ten o'clock he had exhausted his reach-me-down knowledge of the private lives and habits of the Royal family and was relieved when the white-haired captain suggested moving on to a discotheque.

'How about you, squire?' demanded the pilot, pawing Blake on the shoulder. 'Fancy a little go-go-go with the Go-Go girls?'

Blake shook himself free.

'I'm more the stay-at-home kind.'

'With the delectable Denise.'

'She seems a nice girl.'

'She's like the proverbial iceberg. Ten percent frosty show; but believe me, brother, there's fire down below.'

'I can take care of myself.'

'Sure; but can you take care of her?'

'I'll send you a tape-recording.'

Blake made to move away, but found the pilot's whisky-fumed face thrust into his.

'She's the virgin queen, mind you, compared with t'other. Know what we call Freda? The flying mattress. Know why we call her that? Because anyone can get on top of her!'

He laughed jaggedly; only stopped when he was snared by a sooty-eyed blonde with arms like lariats and hauled into the corridor, the lift, the crowded boudoir of the night.

'Well,' said Denise in a quiet voice at Blake's side. 'You were "quite the smash hit".'

'Put it down to my masculine virility.'

'Put it down to being British.'

'Snob.'

She stroked the front of his shirt.

'Blame me?'

With the guests gone and the party over, they sat on a couch drinking white wine and nibbling strips of smoked salmon. Stretched out on the floor before them, Clancy and Freda kissed uninhibitedly – their tongues darting like pink fish from bowl to bowl. It was like watching a live sex show, and Blake heard his breath coming harsh and fast. He tried hiding it from Denise, but she edged nearer, her eyes hazing, her finger tickling his palm.

'She's a blatant exhibitionist,' she murmured. 'She gets a charge out of turning people on.'

'Slandering little me?' said Freda, pulling away from Clancy and leaning her head backwards.

'Cockpit Clara, woman's gift to the flight crews.'

'Jealous?'

'Not with Paul here.'

'Then get him to join the club. Mine is.'

'What club?' Blake enquired.

'The most exclusive in the world.'

The redhead twisted towards him. In her loose emerald green sari she appeared flabbier and more bow-chested than before. Her flesh had a lifeless, alabaster sheen to it, as though it had been grafted on. He felt that if he dug his fingers into it it would disintegrate like rotten fruit. An instinct, a jabbing criminal instinct, told him the evening was just about to pay off.

'Must one be proposed and seconded?' he asked.

'Naturally.'

'And what's it called, this exclusive establishment?'

'The Five Mile High Club. Membership is open only to those who have made love flying at thirty thousand feet.'

'And you're both members?'

'I am. Denise still has to qualify.'

He managed not to look at Clancy. He didn't trust them not to raise their thumbs or cheer.

'I'm initiating your friend on Friday,' she continued.

'Whereabouts?'

'Somewhere over the Congo.'

'I meant whereabouts on the plane?'

'Where would you think?'

He took time to consider.

'Well,' he said finally, 'the cabins are out, so are the lobbies and aisles. That only leaves the galleys.'

She shook her head. 'Still too public.'

'All right; I give up.'

'The cargo hold, of course.'

'First-class?'

'What else!'

He smiled and tipped his glass to her.

'To the new member.'

CHAPTER TWENTY-EIGHT

The telephone shrilled early the next morning – goaded its way through his sleep, bored, and chivvied into his mind. He tried to ignore it – couldn't, and groped a hand towards the insistent receiver. He didn't want the bickering to awaken Bart and deny him the rest he needed.

'Leave it,' hissed someone urgently. 'It's for me!'

A girl reached across him and picked up the nearer of two instruments and spoke in an intimate, confidential voice. They were lying – this stranger and he – between cool, pastel-striped sheets, with sunlight filtering palely through the venetian blinds opposite. He had no clothes on, although his companion wore a transparent polkadot nightdress that ended at her flat, unmarked stomach. As she spoke (she seemed to be challenging something), her right breast tipped against his face. The nipple was erect, thrusting; a hard brown berry eager to be chewed. He moved sideways, eased his head along the pillow, inhaled the singed coffee smell that assailed him, the duty-free perfume of sex.

'If you're accusing me of theft,' said Denise angrily, 'then I shall report the fact to the union. . . . Yes, I'll be there at noon. With my lawyer!'

She scowled and clashed down the off-white receiver.

'Nosy cow!'

'Who was that?' he asked awkwardly.

'An airline supervisor. Prying into last night's party.'

'A morals' enquiry?'

'Worse. She wants to know where the loot came from.'

'How did she hear about it?'

'Someone must have sneaked.'

'Is it serious?'

She relaxed and lay back beside him, her hair silking his shoulder.

'For a first offence, no more than a warning.'

'And after that?'

'Suspension, dismissal. Depends how short-staffed they

are. With a strike on I imagine sentence will be postponed.'

'It's not the first time you've looted the galley?'

'Christ, no! All the stews are on the take. Sometimes the supervisors stop us before we leave the plane – make us turn out our purses and pockets. Freda's had her girdle searched twice.'

'Her *girdle*!'

'The soops robbed the airline bare in their flying days. They're wise to "every female hiding place".'

'Takes one to catch one.'

'Even worse are the stew-spies they plant on us. When that happens you open your next pay packet and find a chic little pink slip inside.'

'Goodbye career.'

'Hello crime.'

He looked keenly at her. She was lying quite still, her arms laid neatly by her sides, a miniature crusader on its tomb.

'You admire criminals?'

'Don't most girls?'

'Not the ones I know.'

'You should get around more.'

'To strange-sounding places.'

'With no extradition laws.'

'I'm a journalist, not one of the great train robbers.'

'You could have fooled me.'

'Ronald Biggs in disguise.'

'Now there's a man I could really go for!'

'Why?'

'Resourceful, positive. Not afraid to put two fingers up to society.'

'You'd help someone like that?'

'I did – once.'

'Where is he now?'

'His present address is care of John Vorster Square.'

'Where?'

'The local tronk.'

'Cosy.'

She shrugged and lit a cigarette from a pack on the bedside table. The lighter and enamelled ashtray were both marked CAC.

'See that telephone – the red one?'

'Yep.'

'That was Rod's. He was in residence before I met you.'

'I'm in transit, remember?'

'Rod began as a one-night stand. They all do.'

'I must borrow his razor.'

'Feel free.'

'And make a 'phone call.'

'Are you trying to shame me, Paul?'

'Could I?'

'When a stew lives with someone, she has her own 'phone installed. That way the airline never hears a man answering when they ring up. If they do, they immediately assume that you're married.'

'How naïve.'

'Usually I ignore it, and do this.'

She sat up, leaned on her elbow, lowered her lips to his chest. Her mouth opened and sucked at his skin like some plump and greedy animal. Down it wriggled, down towards his stomach, gaining strength and nourishment on the way. Warmly over his navel. . . . He shut his eyes, his entire being engulfed by her. On, on, till at last at her insistence there came a bursting, thunderous wave of passion that snatched him from where he was, threw him spent and panting on a beach he had never seen or been to before.

Denise rolled silently away from him, her face flushed, congested, her lips moist.

'Did you enjoy that?'

'It was . . . unique.'

'Didn't your wife do it to you?'

'No.'

'Why not?'

'She thought it . . . perverted.'

'No wonder you divorced her.'

'Shall we make love now?'

'If you want to.'

'Don't *you*?'

'Paul.'

'Yes?'

'You're a "very attractive man". More attractive than you realize.'

'Thank you.'

'You don't have to beg for anything. It's me who should do the pleading.'

'Ask.'

'Go down on me.'

She curved her back, and guided him towards her.

'Shouldn't we save this?' he said.

'For what?'

'The Five Mile High Club.'

'First you must practise.'

She urged him onward, in ways that Karen had never permitted him to enter.

CHAPTER TWENTY-NINE

Afterwards they showered together and made love leaning against the green tiled walls of the bathroom. Less than a yard away he heard Clancy as he awoke and tuned the radio to *Favourites From the Classics*. The running water and the *Capriccio Italien* muffled Denise's startled yelps of delight. She shooed him out of the flat as soon as they were dressed, and wouldn't let him see or talk to Clancy.

'It's against the house rules,' she said, reading from a list of 'operating regulations' pinned on the inside of the front door. 'Clause four: No stew will be interrupted while entertaining in the privacy of her own bedroom. Penalty for offenders: R2.'

'Ring me later,' she whispered as they kissed goodbye in the hall. 'If there's no reply, you'll know the inquisition has got me.'

'Then what?'

'I'll see you this evening – at the airport.'

From one o'clock onwards he rang her hourly. But her telephone – the cream one that was hers – didn't answer. *You're a very attractive man. More attractive than you realize.* Her words clogged his mind like the chorus of some nostalgic tune as he dead-marched through the afternoon, the sun pressing down on his skull like a fiery gold plate.

Shopping in the OK bazaars, he bought a selection of games and novelties for the boys, some see-through lingerie for Karen, then sprawled in The Oscar cinema in Plein

Street watching a South African film called *Breekpunt*. He left the cinema midway through the performance and reached the hotel shortly after four. He let himself into the suite and almost stumbled over Clancy, locked on the floor in one of his yoga positions. Exhaling laboriously he disentangled his body and levered himself to his feet.

'Where you been?' he asked sharply. 'The brains has b'n askin' for you all day.'

'The bioscope,' Blake answered. 'If it concerns you.'

'We *are* goin' native. You'll be calling blacks non-Europeans next!'

Blake ignored him and took the gift-wrapped parcels into the bedroom.

'Where *is* Bart?' he queried, as Clancy followed pulling a sleeveless robe over his leotard. 'You should be with him!'

'You wanna nursemaid, then contact an agency.'

'Anything could happen to him.'

'A three-way split is richer than a four.'

Automatically, Blake's fists knotted and bunched. Clancy swung his body lazily, his face screwed in an arrogant grin.

'You're too knackered to fight,' he sneered. 'You're not used to charvering.'

'Shut up!' Blake cried, positioning himself to strike.

'Go ahead, mate. I could service both them birds and settle you with me foot.'

As he spoke, he lifted his right leg ready to kick Blake in the groin. Both men hesitated; then Bart said behind them:

'If you *must* imitate Humphrey Bogart, I suggest you wait until you are back in London and can watch late night TV.'

Blake opened his fists and relaxed.

'Suits me.'

'It'll keep,' shrugged Clancy.

Bart walked between them, lowered himself onto the couch.

'I have news for you, gentlemen,' he said ominously. 'I have been out and changed my ticket.'

'Ticket?' queried Blake.

'My plane ticket. I am flying back with you both tonight – on the same 747.'

'But *why*?'

'Because, my dear Phil, I need to be more involved in the job. In the actual mechanics.'

'You planned and put it in motion. Isn't that enough?'

'Normally, it would be. But – due to cardiac and other reasons – this will be my last caper. I therefore want to be in the centre of the action. Not feeling its ripples from afar.'

'I don't get it,' said Blake, standing over him. 'You could be in South America by the time the police tie you in on the job.'

'Nagged by the fear that some paid dago was about to drug me, drive me across the border, hand me over to the fuzz. No, my friend. Spiritually you're arrested a hundred times a day in countries where British law can't touch you. Besides, I'm too old to run any more. And too sick even to want to. My cousin's hotel is far enough for me.'

Blake ridged his forehead.

'How about me with a wife and two kiddies? Where do I take them?'

'Does your wife know why you're really here?'

'No, but she soon will.'

'Then you must be honest with her. Present her with a definite and clear-cut choice.'

'To stay with me, or quit.'

'Once that is resolved, you only have your destination to decide upon.'

'Where would you go on my passport?'

'Nowhere.'

'Another three guests for your cousin.'

'Better still, remain in Cape Town.'

'Seriously?'

'Once you've returned the diamonds to Petersen, and the money is banked in Switzerland, you'll be safer here than you would be in Paraguay with the war criminals.'

CHAPTER THIRTY

'You're quite sure the girls are fixed?' asked Bart a couple of hours later, as the airline bus swung off the freeway and cruised towards the low glass-fronted buildings of Jan Smuts Airport.

Blake started and looked up from the magazine he was reading. 'Positive,' he grunted. 'As Clancy discovered, they're both a couple of goers.'

'They'll need to be.'

'Relax, will you? Leave it to us.'

The bus jolted to a halt beside the passenger entrance, and Bart parted contact until they teamed up again at the Tudor Court Hotel. Blake rejoined Clancy, walked with him towards the barriers where the customs and passport officials were waiting with dead underwater eyes and drowned faces.

'You got the stuff well hid?' muttered Clancy nervously.

'In my trusty grip.'

He swung the airline bag buoyantly, as though it contained nothing more lethal than socks and a change of underwear. The phials of LSD which Bart had given him were concealed in a shirt – tucked into the cuffs, to be shaken out when needed. The man who examined his passport was more interested in his views on South Africa than in any drugs he might be carrying. 'Be sure and give your readers a fair picture of us,' he warned. 'And if I don't?' The official snipped his fingers in the air. 'More work for the censor.'

Despite this Blake was sweating heavily when he reached the gate where the rest of the London-bound passengers were congregated. Unlike the outward flight, there were some three or four hundred people herded into listless. docile groups, like holiday-campers awaiting their guides, He looked for Denise and saw her posted between Freda and a steward with wavy chestnut hair and petrified side-burns. She raised a gloved hand to him, excused herself to her companions, came over with the elaborate walk – one foot placed across the other – that she'd been trained to use.

'Good evening, Mr Bennett,' she said coolly. 'And how did you enjoy your stay in Johannesburg?'

'Very much. Except for this afternoon.'

'You had nowhere interesting to go?'

'No-one interesting to go with.'

'I'm sorry about that.'

'I did telephone a friend, but she was out.'

'You know what we South African girls are like.'

'Tell me.'

'Always on the go – changing jobs, seeking new careers.'

'Voluntarily?'

She chewed her lower lip.

'Sometimes we're . . . obliged to.'

'Perhaps that's what happened to my friend.'

'Yes, Mr Bennett. I expect it was.'

'I'd like to hear about it from her.'

'I dare say she'll be "in touch".'

She smiled, cuddled her clipboard to her chest, minced back to the gate. There was no further delay and they filed out to the plane on which the diamonds were already stowed – snuggled in its belly like infants waiting to be born. Only in their case, thought Blake, prematurely.

They were three hours out of Johannesburg before Denise and Freda had satisfied the demands of the travellers in first-class. During that time they had been as rushed, gracious, helpful and efficient as hostesses at a fund-raising party. Drinks had been dispensed without fluster or accident; a rich four-course dinner served, eaten and digested; chocolates brought round; information given about the wide-screen movie to be shown; preparations made for those who wanted to turn in early, and wake up in London at breakfast-time. 'Tea or coffee, sir?' asked Denise when she came to take Blake's morning order. Neither, he told her; keeping the reason, and its importance, to himself.

Outside, the first layers of night blanketed the Boeing as Blake and Clancy made their way to the upstairs bar. They passed Bart dozing awkwardly in his chair, his head slumped against the forward-view window. Blake was worried about the moisture which lathered the accountant's face, dripping from his chin onto the lapels of his gabardine suit. Moving on he greeted the passengers in the friendly way people adopt when they're in the air. He nodded amiably to the four men playing pinochle; winked at the porcelain-cheeked little girl clambering over her mother; retrieved the emergency landing instructions dropped by the lady with the opaque, twitching eyes. All the while observing, cataloguing, appraising – looking for the one man who could blow the whistle on them.

He kept his deductions to himself until Freda had served their brandies at a mosaic side table.

'Well,' he said quietly. 'Which one is he?'

Clancy sipped his drink.

'Odds on the ginger-haired one – with the attaché-case strapped to his wrist.'

'Almost,' Blake allowed. 'He in fact is a courier. But not an armed guard.'

Clancy glanced at him in alarm.

'You know him?'

'The type – not the individual.'

'Who's *your* bet, then?'

'I'd put my money on the tall fellow at the back, the one who only drinks fruitjuice.'

'He's too square. It must be the crew-cut joker – who keeps on chatting up the birds.'

'You're both quite wrong, you know.'

Blake looked up and matched Denise's grin with his own. She had come up behind them, the spikes of her heels sinking silently into the carpet.

'We're playing guessing games,' he explained.

'Healthier than booze.'

'I bet my friend a rand I could pick out the armed guard.'

'Then you'd better pay him.'

'How close was I? Hot, lukewarm, or cold?'

'Below freezing point. That's your party at the opposite table. The one who looks like a college professor.'

He followed her gaze and inspected the thin, narrow-chested man with the lank iron-grey hair, thick-rimmed glasses, and questing nose. He was bent over a file of documents, scribbling notes in the margins.

'If you're both so bored, I've a suggestion to make.'

'We're listening.'

'I know a "chic little club" you can join.'

'Both of us?'

'Singly and one at a time.'

'Who goes first?'

She levelled a coral-nailed finger at Clancy.

'He does. I'm saving you for Later.'

Clancy smirked and got to his feet.

'After you, sir,' said Denise, ushering him forward.

As they left the lounge, Blake saw the guard eye them while squaring-off his papers. He was an experienced professional, wise to most of the tricks and gambits. Even so, Blake hoped to teach him some new ones before they landed at Heathrow.

CHAPTER THIRTY-ONE

'Do you mind if I join you?'

His voice was as stiff and correct as his appearance, and Blake could muster no legitimate reason for refusing him.

'By all means,' he replied. 'You're not interrupting anything.'

The security guard smiled his thanks and sat in the chair Clancy had vacated.

'I gather your friend has found company in the cabin?'

'Looks like it.'

'It can get somewhat lonely, flying at night on one's own.'

'Yes; but you get used to it.'

'Flying, or travelling on your own?'

'Both.'

'Ah, so you're a seasoned traveller.' He removed his glasses and polished the right lens. 'I thought I'd seen you before on this line.'

'I doubt it. This is my first time on CAC.'

'Somewhere else, then. In the City, perhaps.'

'I work in Fleet Street.'

'A journalist.'

'Travel writer.'

'Really! Yet this is your first trip to South Africa?'

'I'm usually more patriotic.'

'I don't quite—'

'And favour BOAC.'

The plane dipped suddenly, like a car going over a hole in the road, and Blake tensed his body. After a moment the Boeing righted itself and he glanced at the guard, whose posture had not changed.

'What field are *you* in?' he asked defensively. 'Or is this a pleasure jaunt?'

'I would that it were.' The man put his spectacles back on and patted the file by his side. 'I'm an assessor – which involves me in an infinite amount of paper work, some of it done at great heights.'

He gave a dry academic laugh, and Blake smiled along with him. They said nothing more and listened to the high sustained whine of the jet's engines, the occasional shudder that ran like a pulse through the fuselage.

'Ah!' exclaimed the guard abruptly. 'Here comes your friend now.'

Blake turned and saw Clancy strutting towards them. The Cockney checked his stride as he noticed the guard, but came on again without displaying concern. Blake cleared his throat to make the introductions, but the 'assessor' jackknifed from the seat.

'I won't impose on you any longer,' he said. 'Some people read a chapter of a book before finding sleep. My soporific is a few minutes' civilized conversation – no insult intended, naturally.'

'And none taken.'

'I bid you both goodnight, then.'

'Till breakfast.'

He dipped his head and walked zestfully to the staircase, the seat of his trousers shiny and notably thin.

'What did *he* want?' asked Clancy, sitting down again.

'As he said. A chat at bedtime.'

'Is that all?'

'Plus some personal information. Which I freely and convincingly gave.'

'Let's hope he's as dim as he looks.'

'He's not, but forget about it. Tell me how you got on.'

'Like always.'

'You joined the club?'

'Life membership.'

'And our objective?'

'B1.'

'It's fixed?'

'Just help yourself.'

'Where's Freda gone?'

'Restin'.'

'And Denise?'

'Up front in the flight deck. She says for you to go down to the bay. She'll join you when she's free.'

'Okay. Wish me luck.'

'It's not luck you need. It's expertise.'

Blake padded down the stairs and into the walk-through galley. At that time of night he'd expected it to be empty; to his dismay the steward with the pompadour hair-do was perched on one of the jump seats, drinking from a plastic container.

'Hi,' the steward said in a soft, lisping voice. 'You're early.'

Blake glanced behind him to the door leading to the underpart of the plane. He shifted his gaze to the cabin, where the passengers were reclining in their seats as if they'd been knocked-out and dumped there.

'Miss Van Heerden isn't here yet?'

'Another half-hour. Come back later if you like.'

'That's all right. I'll wait.'

'Saw you at the girls' party, didn't I?'

'I was there.'

'You didn't see me?'

'Not that I remember.'

'I was in drag.'

'Drag?'

He swung his body like a mannequin showing off a gown.

'A nifty black cocktail number with a single string of Ciro pearls.'

'There were so many—'

'I agree, pet. *Not* the most intimate of affairs.'

'Apparently not.'

'You mean the informer?'

'Yes.'

'Putrid bitch – whoever he was.'

'Is Miss Van Heerden in trouble?'

'Depends how you view it. If you call working your notice trouble, then she's in it up to here.' He placed a manicured hand beneath his chin.

'I didn't know.'

'She'll tell you all the sordid circs. But it'll cost you.'

'Pardon?'

He drained the container, dropped it in a pedal-worked disposal bin.

'You don't think we're going to get away with it, do you?'

'Who?' Blake asked testily. 'Get away with what?'

'All of us who were their guests. The ice queen and the flying mattress will have the knickers off us before they're through.'

'But that's absurd. They in*sis*ted that my friend and I went there.'

'They're a vengeful pair. Especially Van Heerden. Don't let that fey act of hers fool you.'

'Thanks for the warning.'

'Don't thank *me*. Pray to whoever it is you pray to.'

He got up and headed back down the plane.

'I've a midnight rendezvous with a butch old queen with pincers for fingers. If you get bored there's a magazine there you can look at. Highly instructional, it is, and banned in good old SA.'

He pointed to a magazine – *Gayboy* – lying on the aluminium sink, open at the centre-spread. The coloured picture was of a full frontal male nude. Blake waited until the steward had shimmied from sight. Then he turned towards the two urns – one for coffee, the other for tea – which were filled and ready to be heated eight hours later for breakfast. He unslung the CAC grip from his shoulder, took out the two phials of LSD. He laid them on top of the magazine and lifted the lids from the urns. He poured in no more of the drug than would fill a liqueur glass; a measure in each of the vessels. Watched it mingle with the brown tea and darker brown coffee. The operation took no more than twenty seconds. With the empty phials back in their hiding-place, he opened the connecting door to the luggage bay – his heart nagging like an old debt.

CHAPTER THIRTY-TWO

It was hot, dark and cellar-like in the luggage bay. A wire-covered red light, set flush in the ceiling, gave the impression that the hold was on fire, and he inched warily forward as if the narrow corridor was about to splinter and collapse beneath his feet. He passed by the holds containing the passengers' cases and located the space – B1 – in which lay the mailbags. He pulled open the hold which Clancy had unlocked, saw them stacked tightly there like the black plastic rubbish sacks one sees in London shop doorways at night.

At first sight they appeared equally soiled and worthless. Then he tugged them out – all five of them – ignoring those that were crammed to the top, seeking the half-full ones which held the registered mail. There were two, both marked with the distinctive Post Office seal, and he knelt before them as though worshipping at a secret and costly shrine.

The lack of proper light didn't worry him, and he closed his eyes as he grasped the nearer of the bags. He wanted to get the feel of the canvas, its texture and toughness, and slid his fingers down the empty neck to where the seal was in position, throttlingly tight. It would be easy just to slit the bag from neck to bottom, pull out the diamonds parcels, and leave safely before Denise arrived. But that way the theft would be obvious to anyone who made a routine check. His four years at White Star had taught him how the professionals worked; he could not afford to be any less thorough.

His fingers reached forward and took hold of the seal. It was rough and cold in his grasp and tore at the skin as he forced it upwards. The hands which had inconvenienced and humiliated him in the past redeemed themselves as the seal, slowly and reluctantly, began to move.

He let go of it with his left hand and tugged experimentally at the folds of the canvas. That quickened the process, and he ignored the pain invading the fingers that strained and pressed on the device. Now that the seal was finally giving, he opened his eyes and flinched at the redness covering his fingers. For a moment he thought they'd been tinged by the light; but the blood streaked wetly down onto his knuckles, zigzagged across his palm and wrist.

He halted and stemmed the blood with his handkerchief. He knotted the material over his hand and attacked the seal as though uprooting something from the ground. It gave another three inches, then screwed sideways and lodged in a bend in the canvas. He paused and looked at the phosphorescent pointers of his watch. Fifteen minutes had gone already. If it wasn't the right sack he'd be forced to disembowel the other one and bargain on no-one examining it until it was off the plane and in the mail shack.

There was no time for subtlety. He stood, jammed a foot on the bottom of the sack, grasped the seal with both hands. He pulled, waited, pulled again. There was a scraping, rending noise and the seal shot to the neck, where the cord sewn into the rim stopped it going over the end. He put his fingers to his mouth, sucked the fresh blood from them, took out his pocket knife. The blade was sharp enough to shave with, and he used it to make a slit inside one of the topmost folds deep enough to fit his hand through.

His fingers went down through the bag, snatching at air, and then fastening on the uppermost parcels. He quested for a small tin box – smaller than the rest of the registered items – cluttered with official seals. At last, after discarding the bulky parcels housing valuables that were not valuable enough, he touched what he wanted.

He manoeuvred his arm like that of a crane in an amusement arcade; edging, nudging, encouraging the prize towards the mouth of the machine. Suddenly, with a win-or-lose sweep of the crane, he had the object in his clutch and out in the open. He unclasped his hand and saw the simple green label that meant diamonds were inside. He angled the knife to prise a corner of the tin. He thrust his forefinger inside, felt the soft white tickle of cotton wool, knew he'd done what any insurance company would give odds against: *he'd lifted the tomfoolery in mid-air.*

The tin was larger than most, some four or five inches long, and two inches deep. There was enough wealth there to see him through several lifetimes. But he still needed the rest of the boxes. He slipped the tin into his grip and searched the bag for its companions. He estimated there should be six altogether, and lost all sense of caution as he scrabbled in the bottom of the sack. He scooped the cartons out one by one, stood there laughing mutely.

Again he consulted his watch. The full half-hour was up, and he worked on forbidden time as he disguised the slit he had made. He tucked the cut area inside the folds and creases of the canvas, pushed down the seal until it jammed again in the middle of the sack.

That done he returned to the galley, rinsed his hands beneath the tap, and waited on a jump-seat for Denise to arrive. To welcome him to the club.

CHAPTER THIRTY-THREE

He knew he would never forget those hours: sitting erect in the plane, homing in on London airport, with three million stills' worth of diamonds in a cheap canvas grip on his lap. Beside him Clancy shot tight-eyed glances at the bag, as though it held a timebomb which could explode at random. It would only take an overhelpful steward, clumsiness on Blake's part, the built-in suspicion of someone at customs and immigration control, for the mechanism to detonate and blast them to imprisonment for life.

Across the aisle he saw Bart wake up as though emerging from a coma. He straightened his adjustable seat, sponged his face, slipped another nitroglycerine tablet beneath his tongue. The time by Blake's watch was 07.30. Already Denise and Freda were coming round with a light breakfast of fruit juice, rolls, tea or coffee. After their early morning lovemaking in the cramped, vibrating corridor, she appeared flushed and emotionally well-nourished. In contrast to their first antics, their coupling had been as conventional as any of his sessions with Karen. She lay down and guided him straight into her; they used their mouths only for kissing.

When it was over, she confessed to having a 'real lovers' orgasm, way deep inside me'; rewarded him with kisses as light and fragrant as pollen. 'But remember,' she said teasingly. 'You still owe me.'

'More than I can repay.'

'Then start by taking me out to dinner tonight. Somewhere chic and "madly expensive".'

'I don't—'

'Unless you've already got a date. With your ex-wife or mistress – or girlfriend?'

'There's no-one.'

'Then I nominate the Rib Room. They serve the hottest horseradish in London.'

'What time?'

'Eight for eight-thirty.'

'In the bar.'

She nodded. 'Don't forget to book. And be there, won't you?'

'Yes,' he lied. 'At seven fifty-nine.'

A sharp dagger of conscience recalled his promise as Denise stood over him with a tray. She gave a wistful, solicitous smile, a cigarette girl in a night-club. 'Your breakfast, sir. Grapefruit juice, toast, and coffee.' He quickly made room on his knees for the tray, thanked her, heard Clancy brusquely refuse her wares. Her politeness remained as fixed as a permanent wave. She crossed to the security guard, who took only coffee – black, and a large cup of it.

From his research Blake knew that a short period of boiling would not destroy the LSD in the liquid. But he was unsure how long it would be before the drug took effect. Bart had put it at anything from five to thirty minutes, depending on the person and the degree of concentration.

'Some people can brush their teeth with it, and take a trip,' he'd told him. 'Others need a junky's slug before they send for the straitjacket.'

He wasn't concerned who drank how much of what. Or thought he wasn't until he saw Denise nearing the small girl and her mother – who were seated up front, in the nostrils of the plane. Children were something he hadn't calculated for. He couldn't allow the kid to take acid.

Equally he couldn't rush up to Denise and knock the serving pots from her grasp.

Without a word he thrust the tray and grip at Clancy, and strode hurriedly forward. The youngster dawdled on the arm of her seat, watching her mother massaging her forehead, coaxing the wrinkles beneath the brim of her hair.

'Hello,' he said, getting down on his haunches. 'We haven't met yet.'

'Hi. Are you the captain?'

He traded grins with her mother.

'Do I *look* like the captain?'

'Who knows? He's just an incorporeal voice.'

'Takes after her father,' put in the woman proudly. 'He's an American Professor of English.'

'No,' Blake answered. 'I'm not exactly the captain. But I do have a message from him for you.'

'Tell! Tell!'

'He wants you to have a glass of milk with him – compliments of the line.'

'No fooling?'

'Cross my heart and hope to fly.'

'We *are* flying, stupid!'

'That proves it. Milk it is, young lady.'

He stood and turned to Denise, hovering beside them.

'One glass of cow-champagne for Miss Pigtails.'

'And for you, madam?' asked Denise.

'I dunno. I guess I'll–'

'Make that two glasses of cow-champagne. So good for the complexion.'

'Thank the captain for me,' said the little girl as he moved away.

He regained his seat and watched the north of France, the Channel, the sliding English coast unfold beneath him. There were only ten minutes left before landing; already the jet engines were changing their pitch, sounding thinner and meaner, like a tin man belching.

So far no-one had come under the influence of the LSD, and he wondered if it was too weak, if he hadn't used enough of it. He gripped his kneecaps and visualized what could happen if the drug didn't work. The diamond theft could be discovered the moment the cargo came off the hydraulic lift or conveyor belt. If that occurred they'd get no further than the terminal before the police stopped them, along with every other passenger on the flight. Even if the bags reached the mail shack without incident the . . .

'Haw-haw-haw-ha-hee-hee-hoh-hoh-ha-hee-hoh-ha-ha-hee-hee-hee-haw—'

It was like a lunatic braying; a cackling crazy-house figure – inhuman, hellish; freezing the skin, icing the blood.

It came from the man who'd forced himself on Blake the previous night. He lumbered upright, his lips buckled in a sick copy of a grin. He staggered forward, his arms flailing and pushing back the air, as though walking under water. He lurched towards the vertical windows. Reached one and began clawing at it, beating his head against it. He didn't say anything – even when the blood made cracks in his brow, traced red tendrils on the pane. He continued to giggle, to scratch and belabour the Perspex. Finally, when it wouldn't splinter or give way, he propped himself against a seat, screaming:

'I'm a bird! A beautiful, feathery bird! I can fly – just like Daedalus! Let me fly, you bastards! LET ME FLY!!'

After a moment, he straightened up again, retreated to the aisle, put his arms out like a six-year-old playing at aeroplanes. Laughing, cursing, shrieking obscenities, he zoomed up and down the cabin, round the nose of the fuselage and down its flanks. He made engine noises, pretended to stall, gained power and height again. All the while laughing . . . laughing . . . laughing.

At first the shock of watching him made Blake forget about the rest of the travellers. Then two of them, a stout middle-aged woman and a man with bifocals, also stood up. They lowered their heads and charged, bull-like, at the dove-grey walls of the cabin. Another man – pot-bellied, balding – dropped to his hands and knees, scuttled about barking and yapping, snapping at ankles.

A lacquered expressionless blonde in purple stretch pants and lilac halter put her nails to her cheeks and raked savagely downwards. 'Whore!' she screeched viciously. 'Universal *whore*!'

Instantaneously, there were other people doing other things: walking like hunchbacked dwarfs; frothing at the mouth; shaking; turning blue as if they couldn't breathe; whirling on the spot like teetotums. Blake felt someone tugging at his shoulder, swirled round with his fist primed. It was Denise. 'What's happening!' she gasped. 'For Christ's sake, what's going on?'

He drew her from the aisle.

'They're hallucinating,' he said evenly.

'Hallucinating! From *what*?'

'Probably something they ate.'

'Ate! They've only had bread and rolls!'

'Ever hear of St Anthony's Fire?'

Helplessly, she shook her head.

'It occurred in a village in Southern France in 1951. The inhabitants ate bread that was contaminated by some kind of fungus. They thought they were being eaten alive by dragons, chased by blazing fireballs. Some of them tried to jump out of windows and fly!'

She let out her breath and sagged against him. Her body seemed to have been filleted.

'How long will it last?'

'An hour – a day.'

'Jesus! What am I going to *do*?'

'Radio ahead to London. Ask for ambulances and doctors to be standing by.'

She hesitated, stared desolately into his face.

'Hurry!' he urged. 'Before you've a massacre to explain!'

The scene at Heathrow was like a rehearsal for doomsday. Sirens, airtugs, ambulances, fire engines, police, doctors, nurses, stretchers, jubilant members of the Press.

As the medicos entered the Boeing, running like rugby players making a touchdown, those passengers who were fit and unaffected were allowed to leave. They were swallowed up by the Superstair 300, nuzzled against the door like a huge fawn worm. At the end of the stairs they were assailed by hand-held television cameras and stick-microphones which grubbed greedily at their mouths and faces.

Blake looked around, saw that Bart and Clancy had got through unquizzed. He screened his head with the grip, shouldered aside a youthful reporter who tried to detain him.

'BBC, sir,' he began, but Blake was out of questioning range and away.

CHAPTER THIRTY-FOUR

The traffic into London was thick and slow-moving, like a porridge one could hardly stir. The Renault sludged through the insipid western suburbs, past the empty-faced electronics and light-engineering factories, in a frustrating series of stops and goes. In keeping with the plan, Bart and Clancy made their own way to the Tudor Court, by coach and underground. The three men were to meet there by ten o'clock, which gave Blake nearly an hour to deaden as he breached Chiswick, Hammersmith, and came out into the Bayswater Road.

He drove decorously around the park, got stuck in a jam near the Albert Memorial, and was the last to arrive at the hotel. Miss Ridley gestured him upstairs, and he hastened to the bogus fire-door with its ugly steel handle, and the sand-bucket and extinguisher positioned cunningly outside. He knocked, entered, saw Bart lounging at a club footed table draped with a maroon velvet cloth. Clancy stood beneath the half-open skylight, cleaning his nails with a penknife.

'Well,' said Bart brusquely. 'Let's see 'em!'

He slung the bag from his shoulder, unzipped it, and deposited the contents on the table. Bart reached avidly forward, took the first of the green-labelled parcels . . . tore the wrappings from it. The cotton-wool flurried like snow-flakes, and he scattered the gems across the cloth like a gambler throwing dice.

There were ten altogether: flashing violet, green, yellow, ruby-red and blue. The men froze and stared at them as if they might vanish if they took their eyes away. Bart swallowed audibly and picked one of them up. He held it to the light and blinked as needles of blue-white flame lanced his eyeballs.

'Look at the colour,' he crowed. 'The depth, the strength of it! Look at the rainbow it has for a heart!'

He turned the stone so that it refracted the light. The

effect was almost hypnotic, and Blake defensively shook his head.

'What exactly is it?'

'It certainly ain't quartz.'

He swivelled the diamond, showing how the colours were sprinkled throughout it; each one – orange, indigo, red – separated from the next.

'It's gorgeous,' breathed Blake.

'The best, the very best. A "fine blue-white",' Bart murmured, talking almost to himself. 'Cushion-cut and weighing, I'd say, a hundred and thirty carats.'

'So what's it worth?'

'Whatever a collector or dealer will pay for it. One like this, but not as good, went for a hundred and ninety thousand at Christie's in Geneva not long ago. It was a rich golden yellow, a hundred and four carats, and was acquired by Van Cleef and Arpels, the Paris jewellers. Only snag was,' he continued, 'the stone, the so-called Deepdene Diamond, turned out to be a fake. It was examined by the leading gemmological laboratories in Switzerland and England, where it was found to have been "treated" to improve its colour and value.'

'How was that done?'

He fondled the diamond, cupped it between his hands.

'The stone was put under neutron bombardment by electromagnetic radiation. A few years ago it was only the smaller and less precious diamonds that could be recoloured like that. But today it's being applied to larger stones of the hundred carat range.'

'How do we know this isn't a fake?'

'We don't. But I would stake my freedom on it being genuine. The rest are also good. But this is the prize, the beauty. The one you'd choose against the world.'

'Does it have a name?'

'It's waiting to be christened.'

'So let's do so.'

Bart opened his fingers and laid the jewel gently on the table. He smiled at Blake, his voice mocking and low.

'Be careful, Phil. Don't become infatuated with these cold but sexy ladies. They will accept all the devotion and adoration you can give them. And then demand more. They will also send you mad, if you allow them.'

'And in return?'

'You get nothing. They are fickle and faithless. They are like cats, and will go with whoever offers them the thickest cream and the softest pillow.'

'I'd still like to call it something.'

'We shall name it the Blake Diamond, in honour of the man who "discovered" it for us.'

Blake bowed formally, heard Clancy snort with derision. Bart flicked another of the packets towards the Cockney.

'Try this one, Mike, and see what you draw. Put the ones with a yellowish tinge to one side. They are "top crystal"; exquisite, but relatively less valuable. And remember, handle them as you would do a woman, tenderly and with loving care.'

'Thought they was as hard as undertakers' nails.'

Bart shook his head.

'The diamond can be overcome by flame; a single heavy blow can shatter it; it can be cut by a steel blade along any of its cleavage planes. How else do you imagine diamond cutters ply their scrupulous trade?

Clancy didn't answer, and for the next ten minutes they opened the packets, sorted the diamonds according to their size, colour, approximate carat weight and cut. At the end of that time Bart was sweating more than usual. His breathing had become so shallow it was scarcely evident; he held his head as if he was feeling dizzy or faint.

Blake dropped the pear-shaped brilliant-cut he was holding.

'You all right? he said anxiously.

Bart clambered upright.

'Jus' a spasm.'

'Where?'

His lips contorted, seemed to tear themselves from his face. He flapped a hand against his left shoulder.

'Down m'arm.'

He gaped with an expression of shock as though he was in the path of a speeding lorry, and couldn't get out of its way.

Blake started round the table towards him.

'Cold,' he uttered. 'Verra cold.'

Then, as if a second lorry had come up and struck him from behind, he pitched violently forward, dragging the tablecloth and jewels with him. The crash he made as he hit the floor quaked the whole room. There was a grinding noise as the skylight spilled all the way open.

Blake halted, gazed at the accountant's still, diamond-spangled body.

There was no need to feel his heart or pulse.

He was comprehensively dead.

CHAPTER THIRTY-FIVE

Looking back on them, Blake saw that the sixty minutes following Bart's seizure and death were the most significant and decisive of his life. But it was Miss Ridley who, summoned from the reception desk, took control of and minimized the situation. She hurried Clancy and Blake down to the bar and provided a bottle of brandy and two glasses. She disappeared, came back an hour later, and joined them for what she gruffly called a 'snifter'. She raised her glass, drank deeply, and regarded them with small, bloodshot, distrustful eyes.

'Weep and grieve not,' she said. 'It's the way Don would have wanted to go. His whole life was a calculated risk. Therefore it will not be necessary for either of you to attend the funeral. I am his only living relative, and I want it to be purely a family affair. There is, however, the question of what could be termed his will.'

'His will?' repeated Blake.

'Or should I say legacy and last wishes.'

'There's nothing I want—'

'Please wait until you've heard me out, before declining or accepting anything. First of all I must know whether or not you intend carrying the operation to its ultimate conclusion. That is the exchange of the diamonds for money obtained from the chairman of White Star.'

Blake felt Clancy's eyes rayed upon him.

'Yes,' he said firmly. 'I do.'

'Good. Then you will have no objection to dealing with me now, in place of Donald. You can look upon me as your clearing-house, liaison and base. Whatever you entrust to me will be impersonally dealt with and distributed as Don would have wished. I, of course, will assume his role as the fourth partner.'

'Seems practical.'

She grunted her satisfaction.

'In that case we will adhere to the original plan. I will give your colleague here sufficient funds to keep him from treachery and greed until you deliver the major prize. He is free to live in the "guest-room" upstairs, or I have an inn in the country he can be sent to. Safety-wise there is little to choose between them, but the choice is his.'

'Never fancied the country,' said Clancy. 'Too many fences.'

'So be it. That leaves the question of money, fresh identities, and so forth.'

'Just a minute,' Blake interrupted. 'Where does Monkton fit into all this? And where is he now, anyway?'

'He fits in, Mr Bennett, as he always did. His present whereabouts is no concern of yours. But, to show that I am not trying to bluff you, I can reveal that he is on the civilized side of the Irish border.'

'In Eire.'

'Where he will remain until he receives from me his full quarter-share.'

'Providing I get through and deliver.'

She regarded him sharply.

'My cousin's foresight and legacy should ensure that. Although physically he can no longer do so, mentally he always anticipated tomorrow.'

'In what way?'

She reached into her inside jacket pocket (she had on a hairy lemon-and-rust tweed suit) and handed him a thick, business envelope. She watched as he opened it and gazed inside, as if into a kaleidoscope. Included among the documents and money were two blue-bound British passports; one belonging to a Mr H. T. Martin, the other to his wife. There was also a note from Bart, which he took out and pensively read.

My dear Philip,

I hope I'm around to give you these papers myself. If not and you receive them from Martha, don't feel obliged to use them. It's better to be alive and honest than as I am.

I've put your sons on your passport. I thought somehow you would prefer that. As it is the first thing the police will look for, I have not used your own initials this time.

Be happy and live long,

Bart.

He folded the note, put it back in the envelope, gummed down the flap.

'Anything else you need or want to know?' demanded Miss Ridley.

'Just the diamonds.'

'You can collect them from my office. On your way out.'

She rose and marched to the corridor while he said goodbye to Clancy; a surly, eye-averted handshake and grudging 'good luck'. He then followed her into the dingy, glassed-in box that could have guarded the hallway of a Victorian men's club. Outside came the clamour of road-works, as though a dentist was drilling in a giant's jaw.

Miss Ridley stooped over a black-and-grey Chubb safe, took out a suede draw-purse, passed it to him. The jewels moved in his hand like ballbearings.

'I believe these are yours.'

'Ours.'

'Never forget that. It only takes one telephone call, wherever you are, to have you . . . reminded.'

'Bart warned me of that.'

'Of what?'

'Dishonour among thieves.'

She sat while he stowed the purse in his change pocket.

'It was Donald's intention,' she announced formally, 'for you to proceed to Cape Town by boat. That way you could relax until further sins of mankind occupied the front pages. Twelve days on the Union-Castle line is better for you than a month at a health farm. And no more expensive.'

He shrugged and turned to the door.

'I'll be in touch.'

'You'd prefer to fly?'

He paused in the jamb, spoke over his shoulder.

'Only if my wife insists.'

CHAPTER THIRTY-SIX

Despite the urgency and his desire to keep moving, Blake didn't plumb Karen's feelings until the next morning. Their first evening together had been close and emotional, as though they'd been parted for three months instead of three days. She was gladder to see him than he'd expected; and, like sweethearts meeting in the midst of a war, they had drunk and made love too greedily and too much.

In deference to both their hangovers, he picked his moment carefully, over strong eleven o'clock coffee, taken at opposite ends of the couch. He knew better than to broach the subject outright, and waited until she yawned, stretched, gazed lazily at him.

'By the way, darling,' she drawled, 'how was your trip? You still haven't described it.'

He matched her in tone and delivery.

'So so.'

'Profitable?'

'Quite.'

'Going on another one soon?'

'Possibly.'

'It's not only myself I'm asking for.'

'Did the boys miss me so much?'

'More than just them.'

'Who?'

She lit a cigarette, spiralled the smoke out through her nose.

'He left his card on the mantelpiece, behind the clock. Wanted you to ring him as soon as you got home.'

Blake rose, took the card from where it had been tucked. He felt no particular interest in the caller, whoever he was. In spite of the palaver in the papers and on television about 'mid-air drama at Heathrow', there had been no mention of the diamond theft. The security guard was detained in hospital, after diving through a ward window, and doctors were still removing glass from his body, treating him for 'severe blood loss'. By the time De Beers reported the stones' non-arrival to the Post Office, and their journey had been retrospectively checked, he would be resident abroad under the alias of Martin, Howard Timothy.

He looked casually at the oblong piece of pasteboard, disliking the ornate Gothic script. Then he read the actual lettering.

> **Detective-Inspector Frederick Dewhurst**
> **CID**
>
> **New Scotland Yard,**
> **Broadway,**
> **London, SW1**
> **Tel: 01-230 1212**

The card fell from his fingers and he caught it before it cushioned to the ground. He read it again, looked accusingly at Karen.

'Why didn't you tell me about this before?'

'I must have forgotten.'

'Forgotten!'

'Why? Do you know him?'

'Of course I don't.'

'Then why the panic?'

'Don't most people fear the police?'

'Only if they deserve to.'

'What did he want this . . . Dewhurst?'

'To know about you. He asked all kinds of awkward and leading questions.'

'Such as?'

'Where you were at the moment. What you were doing there. What your present employment was. The name and address of the firm. It was as bad as a census form.'

'Was that all?'

'Not quite. He also asked if you knew someone called Mills. Gordon Mills.'

'Never heard of him.'

'Apparently he was a prison officer at Manston. Got himself badly injured trying to stop a convict from escaping.'

'Was? You mean he's dead?'

'As good as. His brain has been permanently damaged. He'll never think or do for himself again.'

'I'm sorry.'

'I thought you would be.'

'But . . . what did you tell this policeman?'

'Certainly not that boloney about Home From Home Holidays.'

'Then what *did* you say?'

'Simply that, after the fiasco of our second honeymoon, we had agreed to a trial separation. You are supposed to be in Scotland, fishing.'

'Did he believe you?'

'He appeared to. He wanted to know what flies you were using. I said the sort you catch trout with.'

She sat back and spread her arms along the top of the couch.

'Well, darling,' she said softly. 'Isn't it time you stopped treating me like a wife? I *know* there's no job as I tried contacting that ludicrously-named agency you're supposed to be with. Tell me what it is you're doing, Phil. Then perhaps I can be a friend to you, and an equal.'

He nodded, sat down, took her hand in his.

'It's a long story and a tall one. You may not believe it. In fact, I'd rather you didn't. Because if you think I'm telling the truth, you could hate me more than I could bear.'

'That's a risk we'll both have to take.'

'You're certain?'

'Certain.'

'Well,' he began hesitantly. 'It all started like this—'

During the next half-hour he told her everything. About Manston, his meeting there with Bart, the firm they had formed with Clancy and Monkton, the job they had decided to pull, the inside information that only he possessed, the rendezvous with Reynolds the chopper pilot, the prison snatch, his drinks with Whitfield, the mission to South Africa, the return flight and how he'd snatched the gems, the business with the LSD, the arrival at Heathrow, Bart's death, the role Miss Ridley had assumed, what he intended doing next to her father and his company.

When he'd finished he thought she would never speak,

would never comment on his confession. Finally, as his eyes became blurred, she made the two clicking noises in her throat that meant she was about to say something important.

'Philip.'

'Yes, Kar?'

'Do you know what I think?'

'Uhuh.'

'I think it's the most fabulous, exciting, *gutsy* thing I've ever heard of!'

He shook himself and looked up at her. She was as flushed and vibrant as a schoolgirl given an unexpected holiday. Three cheers for . . .

'You don't mind it's your father whom I'm—'

'*Mind!* It's something he's had coming to him since I discovered what gender I was. We're loving enemies. But that's not the vital thing, darling. Not the vital thing at all.'

'What is?'

'The fact you've done something so *manly*! Really, Phil, I was beginning to despair of you. But now–'

'Now?'

'How does a subject – a willing slave – address her king?'

'Your Majesty.'

She knelt before him, playful but sincere.

'Command, Your Majesty, and I shall obey.'

CHAPTER THIRTY-SEVEN

The message on the telex arrived the day after Blake changed his identity, and he and his family quit Carlton Close for good. The message, longer than its predecessors, was a mixture of fact, supposition, apology and bluff. The man with the hearing-aid read it rock-faced. When he blinked – a muscle flickered in his cheek – it seemed as if the movements had been chiselled from him.

WEEKLY CHECK REVEALS BLAKE WIFE AND CHILDREN HAVE LEFT COUNTRY STOP VISITED THEIR HOME AND DISCREETLY QUESTIONED NEIGHBOURS STOP STORY IS THEY HAVE TAKEN

THE BOYS ON HOLIDAY STOP ALLEGED DESTINATION TURKEY STOP GAINED ACCESS TO HOUSE STOP FOUND ALL CLOTHES AND VALUABLES GONE STOP POSSIBLE THESE HAVE BEEN STORED DUE TO BURGLARIES IN DISTRICT STOP COULD HAVE FORESTALLED BLAKE BUT FOR ORDERS NOT TO INTERFERE STOP FEEL ANY FURTHER STEPS SHOULD BE TAKEN BY YOU OR INTERPOL STOP AM AVAILABLE IF NEEDED STOP WHITFIELD

As he finished reading, the man with the hearing-aid relaxed, the tension sloughed from his body. Once again Whitfield had given him all he wanted and needed to know. The man was useful, but a fool. He could gather factors together, but was unable to bring unity to them, to weld them into a whole. Holiday . . . Turkey . . . clothes and valuables stored . . . Interpol.

The man with the hearing-aid smiled to himself, balled up the piece of paper, dropped it into a waste basket. He flicked a switch on the bristling intercom on his desk. Waited for a moment then spoke:

'Blake's on his way to us,' he reported jubilantly.

PHASE FOUR

CHAPTER THIRTY-EIGHT

There was no doubt about or denying it: the Howard Martins were the gayest, most active and in-demand couple aboard the *Windsor Castle*. Howard himself – tall, robust and brimming with personality – was a special favourite. Blake met him each morning when he looked into the shaving-mirror, and marvelled at the way they were so unlike. Martin owed a lot (if not everything) to the knowing photographer at Manston who had taken mug-shots of Blake for the prison and Interpol records. 'A word to the wise', he'd said, telling him how to fool and throw off the fuzz.

It had seemed remote and fanciful then – to wear glasses, crop his head, inject liquid paraffin in the bridge of his nose. But before sailing from Southampton he'd done those things. He had the granny glasses fitted by a National Health optician; his hair razor-cut in a Bond Street salon – so close and fine that the red had been completely erased, and the stubble was grey with a fan-shaped bald patch on the crown of his head. The paraffin injection was done by Karen. It hurt less than he'd imagined and broadened the whole centre section of his face, so that his chin seemed almost slight by comparison. With the removal of his beard he felt confident that no one would recognize the late Philip Blake.

Karen entered into the part like the actress she'd once thought of being. She too had her hair cut even shorter and dyed it a rich, burnished bronze. It was a risky thing taking her back to Cape Town, where she'd been born, educated and raised. Her father was still in business there, and her school and university friends were mostly married and living in the fancy southern suburbs between the corner of Devil's Peak and the shores of False Bay.

The years in England, however, had thinned and aged her.

'There's not one of them who'd say "Hi" to me now,'

she boasted. 'You know what they used to call me? "Little Karrie Petersen", with a "K". She was so sweet, plump and eager-to-please she made a cocker spaniel puppy seem anti-social. And stupid! She was as thick as Table Mountain!'

It was with the children, of course, that he had the trickiest problem. How to explain to them that their parents were not mad, doped, or (as they were) on the run. As he was the youngest, Ian was the easiest to hoodwink. Blake spoke with him in the green-carpeted sitting-room of their suite, reviewing the 'game' they were playing.

'It's great fun,' he said. 'Because we're all somebody else now.'

'You're not Daddy?'

'I'm Daddy to you and Alastair. Mr Martin to everyone else.'

'And Mummy; who's she married to?'

'Still to me. She's Mrs Kathy Martin now.'

'Who's Ian?'

'You are.'

'Ian who?'

'Ian Martin.'

'Funny name!'

'You'll get used to it.'

'Daddy.'

'Yes, Ian?'

'Is it like Curlock Shoames?'

'Like who?'

'You *know* – the 'tective on the television serious.'

'Sherlock Holmes.'

'He has dist-guises.'

'That's right, son. Pretend you're Sherlock Holmes in disguise. Only don't tell anyone about it.'

'Not even Dr Waston?'

'Not even him.'

Alastair, when he talked with him on the sun deck, he had to be less frivolous with. He was turning into a grave, logical child. They stood at the rail watching the monotonous slip-slop of the sea, the way the waves broke and re-formed, broke and re-formed against the bottomless pink side of the ship.

'Have you done something wrong, Dad?' the boy asked.

'Some people might think so.'
'The police?'
'Perhaps.'
'What about Mum?'
'What about her?'
'Does she think you're . . .'
'A crook?'
'An outlaw.'
'She wouldn't be with me if she did, would she?'
'Guess not.'
'Well then?'
'Nothing, only . . .'
'Only?'
'Please, Daddy, don't get caught!'

CHAPTER THIRTY-NINE

Apart from social activities in the smoke room, verandah café, and bar, Blake spent most of his time in the gymnasium and health spa. Within a week of leaving England his weight was down to a firm and manageable 210 pounds. Karen appreciated the improvement, especially in bed, and congratulated him on his 'rebirth – the "second coming of Philip Blake".'

It was not until the ninth day out (with Madeira and Las Palmas behind them) that they officially learnt about the diamond theft. Blake sauntered into the lounge for a mid-morning coffee and idly picked up a copy of the *Ocean Mail*. Usually the sheet contained nothing more compelling than weather reports, events of the day and news snippets. But the bald headline HEATHROW DIAMOND ROBBERY: GANG SOUGHT made him shiver despite the even temperature of the room.

The report itself was no more than two paragraphs long. What few facts there were were accurate and unembroidered. It stated that 'three men were wanted for questioning by the police' and ended: 'The investigation is being led by Detective Chief Superintendent Alfred Harvey, and his colleague, Detective Inspector F. Dewhurst – the team responsible for the arrest of the Southampton heroin smugglers last year.'

Blake didn't know how long he sat there, the paper clutched in his hands. He realized nothing until someone eased into the seat next to his, leaned across and said:

'What's the matter, darling? You look as if you've been thrown overboard from a lifeboat.'

'The matter? Just this.'

He handed Karen the news-sheet, watched her face as she read the item. She folded the paper in two, dropped it indifferently on the table.

'What do you think it means?' he asked dully.

'What I think doesn't matter any more. *You* put yourself in the hands of a has-been. Brilliant job! Police baffled by ingenious and elusive mob! That's all tabloid journalism crap. You're as aware as I am that The Great Diamond Robbery was about as brilliant and well-executed as a launderette break-in.

'You got away with this idiotic caper of yours through luck, luck and more good luck. You could have been fouled-up and arrested at any stage of it. Just examine your so-called "firm of four". An elderly cardiac sufferer with more folly than grandeur. A dense north-country thug now stranded in the midst of an Irish civil war. An illiterate Cockney moron who's only good for one thing, and is probably a repressed homosexual anyway. And yourself.

'You're more amateurish than the Great Train Robbers even. And look at the trail *they* left behind them. Fingerprints all over the farm they hid at; telling the neighbours they'd moved in as "decorators"; playing Monopoly to pass the time; "knocking-off" lorry-loads of fruit and vegetables from Covent Garden; sending out for cans of ale.

'Then Biggs, when he'd got his money, pouring a hundred and twenty thousand over his wife's bedroom carpet. High adventure! Folk heroes! Rebels against society and the establishment! A bunch of pinheaded delinquents more like it!

'You forget that I'm a woman, Phil. A married woman with the responsibilities of two growing children. Not a gangster's moll in it for kicks!'

She spoke low and tensely, without raising her voice. There was nothing to suggest they weren't discussing whether or not to dress for dinner, or if they should attend the Ocean Derby.

'Last week you admired what I'd done,' he protested.

'I admired what you did to my father. You paid him back for the way he treated me after mummy died. Lacing me in a straitjacket of position, politics, wealth. But the rest of it – this on-the-run business – it's too bloody wearing! I'm twenty-seven, Phil, and I look forty!'

'What do you want me to do, then? Give myself up? Go to the captain with my hands out in front of me. It would be the most sensational seagoing arrest since Crippen.'

She sighed and, with an abruptness that disturbed him, her features dissolved into dread.

'I can't tell you what to do,' she muttered. 'I only know you seem determined to go through with this thing—'

'Too late now to change ships.'

'— and I'll stick with you until you either—'

'Give myself up or get caught?'

'Is there an alternative?'

'Yes,' he replied fiercely, 'there is. The alternative is for me to carry out Bart's plan to the tee. I'll exchange the diamonds for money, bank it in Switzerland, and then we'll be free to—'

'Run some more.'

'Go somewhere safe and be as peaceful and loving as we can.'

'The book *I* read didn't end like that.'

'What book?'

'*The Robbers' Tale*. It's in the ship's library. Tells all about Biggs and his juvenile antics. I'd get it out if I was you. It's a definitive account of idiocy and woe.'

Later he did as she'd suggested. He agreed with her about the pay-off. A thirty-year sentence in maximum security. But his story wouldn't end that way. He would take real life and give it a fictional conclusion. One that said,

'They lived richly ever after.'

CHAPTER FORTY

The decision to hold a cocktail party in their suite was Karen's and was typical of the exaggerated and capricious way in which she'd started to behave. Her moods alternated between sudden elations (when she praised Blake's criminal inventiveness and nerve), and equally abrupt glooms (the excuse to berate his 'immature greed'.) She announced the party idea on the afternoon before they were to dock.

'It's expected of us,' she explained. 'The done thing. The proper form.'

'No-one else is throwing a party.'

'No-one else is us.'

'What's that supposed to mean?'

'Only that we'd disappoint our fellow passengers if we didn't follow the rules.'

'Rules. What rules?'

'Of this pantomime we are involved in. Haven't you noticed how everyone is intrigued by us. The respectable sizing up the shady.'

'Is that how you think of us – as shady?'

She shrugged. 'I go along with the majority. Why do you think we've been so popular on this voyage?'

'Modesty stills my tongue.'

'They sense something about us – those propped-up pillars of society. Something sinister and bizarre. "How did he make his money?", they're asking. What are he and his family doing on this ship? Where are they *really* going to? What's their *purpose*? What *are* they hiding? What are they *running* from?'

Blake scowled at her, curled up in the chair opposite his.

'Like most of the males on board, I'm a businessman. Equally hardworking and correct.'

'Except that the line you're in is crooked.'

'Retired oilman now engaged in import/export.'

'Importing diamonds.'

'Exporting money.'

She sighed theatrically.

'So that's the end of our party. We're too respectable to have one!'

'Not at all. Go ahead and arrange it. Invite whoever you want. You've cast me in an image, and I'm loath to shatter it.'

Despite the short notice they were given, the staff of the catering office had everything organized and laid-on for six that evening. An hour-and-a-half of gin, vodka, brandy and whisky. The party itself was unremarkable. A dozen or so complacent and gushing matrons in jewels, white furs and silver dresses. Their dinner-jacketed husbands in attendance like so many portly security guards. The boys were also present, guzzling cakes and lemonade, appearing every now and again at knee- or waist-height like jesters at a medieval court.

It was only as seven-thirty neared, and the steward began to unobtrusively check the amount of liquor remaining, that something gave meaning to Karen's manic-depressive behaviour: made Blake realize they were stalking a hairline between survival and discovery.

He had shaken hands with the last guest when the ship's purser entered the suite, stood solicitously at his side.

'Yes,' snapped Blake 'What is it?'

'Excuse me for barging in like this, sir. But there's a little matter I'd like to discuss with you.'

'Anything wrong?'

'No, sir.'

'Then out with it.'

He smiled respectfully, giving Blake the full force of his youth, sun-browned skin, dark pomaded hair.

'I think it would be better if we spoke in my office, sir.'

'Why? I've got nothing to hide.'

'Of course not, sir. But if you would be so good—'

'As you like.'

Leaving the boys in the steward's care, they accompanied the purser to his office on 'C'-deck. He ushered them inside, closed the door and turned smiling towards them.

'All right,' Blake said bluffly. 'You've got us here. Perhaps you'll tell us what it's all about.'

'Certainly, sir. I'm acting under the captain's instructions. He would have liked to be here himself, but unfortunately he's been detained on the bridge. So I shall have to perform his duty for him.'

'Come on, man. Get on.'

'Well, sir, it's like this. We've been checking our records and we find that there's something unusual about your booking. Something quite unusual which we weren't expecting.'

'So?'

'We cabled our chief passenger officer in London, and they told us to go ahead and take the necessary action.'

'Action? You sound as if we've burgled the ship's safe.'

'Far from that, sir.'

He moved away, picked up a stout brown envelope from a mahogany writing-desk. Still smiling, he came back and handed the envelope to Blake.

'With the compliments of Union Castle.'

'What is it. A summons?'

'A free voucher for your return trip.'

'A *what*?'

'Free voucher, sir. We discovered – as our London end *should* have done – that you are the half-millionth passenger to sail with us since our inception in 1900. We weren't expecting the figure to be reached until our next voyage out in October. But as I say, there's been a slip-up, and we are the first to admit it. You will also find a bottle of vintage champagne on your dinner table tonight. Again with the compliments of the company.'

Blake supposed he must have thanked him. But his mind remained scrambled until he reached the dining-room, had the waiter open the bottle of Krug.

He raised his glass, wound his arm through Karen's, drank a loving-cup with her.

'To us, darling,' he said jauntily.

'To us.'

'And a future that can't go wrong!'

CHAPTER FORTY-ONE

After the incident with the purser Blake woke early the next morning, determined to show Karen he was in control of his nerves and their safety. The ship docked at Cape Town at seven, and an hour before that he filled in the declaration form (the DA 303) for the customs officials. Karen also completed one, and it was then, as she came to the clause about full duty being waived on 'worn clothing or jewellery', that she asked about the diamonds; wanted to know how he was going to get them off the ship and into the country.

He had spent much of the voyage considering that, and still hadn't made up his mind.

'You know what these are known as?' he asked, dangling the suede purse in front of her. 'A smuggler's best friend. At 142 carats an ounce what else could they be?'

'Very impressive. But it still doesn't answer my question.'

He squatted on the foot of the bed, swung the purse to and fro like a pendulum.

'Because they're so compact,' he said, 'diamonds have been smuggled in just about everything you can think of. Jars of face-cream and toothpaste tubes. Half-smoked cigars and half-eaten boxes of chocolates. Signet rings, snuff-boxes, golf clubs, umbrellas. . . . The vagina and rectum are also popular.'

'Think of some other places, darling. Unless *you're* looking for a cheap thrill.'

He kept quiet while she finished the packing. He knew he could no longer keep the stones in his spongebag. Too many smugglers had been trapped that way (with the jewels rolled in toy balloons to protect them from the hair-oil in which they were immersed, like coins in a Christmas pudding.) He was still pondering the question when Karen came and sat next to him. She looked very collected and crisp in a beige two-piece suit, and most customs officers would pass her luggage without more than a cursory check.

'What's it to be?' she asked flippantly. 'The body-belt or the false high-heels?'

'Neither.'

'So what *is* the answer?'

'There isn't one. Which is why I've got the stones in my jacket and trouser pockets.'

'How crude.'

'It *should* be more stylish. I'm following in a very stylish tradition.'

'You are?'

'All the greatest diamonds have either been stolen or smuggled, or both. When Queen Victoria accepted the Koh-i-Noor she knew it really belonged to the Rajah of Lahore. It was hidden for years in a turban before being brought to England. The Sancy Diamond, owned for a time by Elizabeth I, was smuggled in the stomach of a corpse. And the Regent Diamond was taken out of India by a sailor who cut a special hole for it in his thigh. Even the Hope Diamond, now in Washington, once dwelt in the folds of a road-sweeper's coat.'

'If *they* swung it, *you* can.'

'No reason why not.'

'We'll bluff our way through.'

'Believe me, darling, we'll walk it.'

Eight o'clock on a bright September morning – the start of the South African spring – standing on the boat deck of a liner entering Cape Town harbour. Blake doubted if there was any more beautiful and exhilarating a sight in the world. He stood with his arm around Karen, inhaling the warm, shining air, widening his eyes at the blueness everywhere: the sky, the sea, the smoke drifting from the city up to the blue sweep of Table Mountain. In front of it the white, tidy buildings came down to the water's edge, waited there like clean and well-groomed beggars too polite to put their hands out.

'Happy homecoming,' he said, as a tug fussed obsequiously around the mailship.

'I never thought it would be like this.'

'You'd forgotten how . . . magnificent it is?'

'I meant my circumstances.'

As they walked down the gangway onto the wharf, over

to the customs hall, Blake listed every trick and try-on. No-one would expect him to smuggle diamonds *into* the country; unless there'd been a tip-off he'd be no more or less under suspicion than anyone else. He'd made sure that neither of the boys carried any toys or cuddly animals, had told Karen not to wear a floral or elaborate hat. He reinspected her as they waited for the officer – wedge-faced and dour – to reach their luggage. His throat somersaulted and changed places with his stomach.

'Those dark glasses,' he hissed urgently. 'Take them off!'

She raised a face that appeared to have no eyes; only two black wounds dwarfing and distorting her nose.

'The light dazzles.'

He put his hand out to snatch them from her.

'There's no need to be violent.'

She removed the glasses and put them in her purse.

'That's better.'

'I still don't—'

He glanced to see if the customs man was watching. The officer was rummaging through a pigskin case belonging to one of the elderly woman passengers. Her cries of outrage rivalled those of the gulls outside.

'It's your eyes they want to examine,' he whispered. 'Much more so than your luggage.'

'But why?'

'To discover the blink rate.'

'The what?'

'Blink rate. People with clear consciences blink no more than twenty or thirty times a minute. These men are experts. They're trained to watch for it.'

'I—'

'It's nervous tension that causes it to change. You're at least a hundred to the minute right now. Calm down and relax. Don't talk too much or too little. Don't wring your hands, and for God's sake stop biting your lips!'

Her poise collapsed, lay around her like shattered glass. She was an obvious target, and because of it he was also. Husbands and wives rarely smuggled independently. They usually formed a team.

'Can I smoke then?' she asked thinly. 'Or is that also taboo?'

She puffed at a cigarette as if taking small fastidious bites out of it. He saw the customs officer approaching, surreptitiously wiped his hands on his trouser seams. Remember, he told himself, not too friendly and not too hostile. Don't gulp and, above all, don't let your voice go falsetto.

The first part of the examination went according to the book. The man scoured the array of cases and finally swivelled his gaze onto Blake. His eyes were the colour of old pennies, and just as lack-lustre and hard. Blake let his own eyes stray to one particular case, a grey one with steel bands and piping. He looked away from it, and back to it; away from it, and back to it. The officer practically choked accepting the bait.

'Do you mind opening this one, sir?'

'If you insist.'

Blake tapped his pockets for the keys, handed them across, impassively watched the search. At last, with nothing more contraband uncovered than Karen's *broderie anglaise* nightgowns, he was allowed to repack the case and leave. He took a cab from the docks, up Heerengracht, to the hotel Karen had chosen near the Malay quarter. They were too involved answering the boys' questions to say much to each other. But shortly before reaching the bronze statue of Van Riebeeck, she hushed them and plucked excitedly at his sleeve.

'That's it right there.'

'That's what?'

'The insurance firm you're interested in.'

He looked back and examined the tall, glass-fronted building. Its doors would soon be open for business, and he intended paying his respects the following morning. To be the most unusual and significant client of the day.

CHAPTER FORTY-TWO

Ideally, he would have preferred to spend more time adapting himself to Cape Town before confronting Petersen. But he refused to make the mistake of thinking that once he was through customs he had got away with it.

Legally, three years had to elapse before he could feel safe. Even then he could be charged and taken to court as long as the goods themselves still existed. He had to get rid of the diamonds – and fast.

He explained that to Karen and left after a light breakfast in the hotel restaurant. He found the layout of Cape Town as direct and simple as a map. Wide boulevards running from top to bottom, with the side streets branching off them like rungs on a ladder. He strode down Buitengracht Street – in which the hotel was situated – right along Wale Street, and on into Adderley Street, the handsome main drag. He was encouraged at the sense of elation he obtained. It seemed to be beamed into him from the sun, a golden gun pointed straight at his chest. The sky radiated blueness as he mixed with the pedestrians who went by him with the same sense of optimism and vigour.

He rounded the grass-ringed fountain that divided Adderley Street from Heerengracht, cut through a row of parked cars, approached the home and head office of White Star Insurance. Seen close to the building was a honeycomb of steel and glass, with the sun and sky mirrored brightly in it. A commissionaire in a cream uniform with light-blue facings looked incuriously at him as he went in through the self-operating glass doors.

He halted in a high marble lobby with open cubicles in which crouched the front office men and minor executives. A blonde slim-legged girl sat at the far end of the hall, at a fibreglass desk set between two silver elevators, behind the doors of which the fires of a crematorium might burn. He moved towards her, conscious of the echoing, chapel-like effect made by his shoes.

She smiled and raised her head as he neared. Her eyes and skin were honey hued. He seemed to have seen her face on fashion magazines on every bookstall.

'Good morning, sir,' she said prettily. 'May I be of assistance?'

'Yes,' he replied, 'you certainly may. I'd like to see Mr Petersen. Mr Theo Petersen.'

Her smile remained steady. 'You have an appointment, sir?'

'No. But I'm sure he'll see me.'

The smile faded a little.

'I'm sorry, sir, but that won't be possible. No one sees Mr Petersen without—'

'I said he'll see *me*.'

The smile vanished.

'If you care to complete this form, I'll send it up to his office. But I fear you'll be wasting your time.'

'Care to bet a few rand on that?'

He took the flimsy green form from her. He laid it on the desk, produced his Parker ballpoint, filled in the necessary details while the receptionist examined her overdeveloped kneecaps. The date; his name (which he gave as 'Smith'); and Object of Interview: 'Urgent insurance business. Return of missing property'. He handed the questionnaire back to her, together with one of the diamonds placed inside a balloon. It was orange, and blown up it revealed a grinning Mickey Mouse head.

'See he gets this as well,' he ordered.

She summoned a messenger boy from an alcove at the back of the hall. The boy entered the elevator bravely, undaunted by the invisible flames.

'Like to take another bet?' Blake asked as they waited. 'That he sends for me within five minutes flat.'

It was a pity for him she wasn't a gambler. The boy returned three minutes later, with instructions to take him to the uppermost floor. He then handed him on, like a baton in a relay race, to a secretary who could have been the twin of the girl downstairs. Without a word she ushered him through an ante-office (electric typewriter, photocopying machine, telex), and into a long teak-panelled room. The inner sanctum, according to the discreet bronze plaque on the door, of: Theo J. Petersen, Chairman and Managing Director.

The girl silently withdrew leaving him alone, although he had the feeling of being spied upon by unseen eyes. He paced around the room, the pile of the camel hair carpet lapping against his ankles. The office was on the corner of the building, with an unbroken view down to the harbour. Petersen's desk was L-shaped, and on it were three ornately framed photographs: a signed one of President Kruger; General Hertzog in braces and a white soft hat, talking to the outdoor staff of a goldmine; and one of Karen, aged about fifteen, standing next to an older woman who had her arm around her shoulder. The youngster's bright, expectant face gazed trustingly out at Blake, and he had a quick surge of guilt – as if he had taken something from her, something fine and individual, which could never be renewed.

He made himself look away from the girl he had spoiled, turned to the near wall, dominated by a cabinet Teljoy set: the nearest thing South Africans have to television, which was installed awaiting transmission of pictures on the empty screen. He stared into it, visualizing the electronic figures that would one day caper across the lines. He didn't hear the side-door open, and someone pad into the room. The first he knew of Petersen's presence was when the South African coughed sharply, and said: 'I believe you have something to offer me?'

CHAPTER FORTY-THREE

Blake was surprised at how small Petersen was – no more than five feet four or five – with everything about him in neat proportion. His eyes were small brown buttons stitched onto a face that was all planes and angles; pointed jutting cheekbones; a chin that dipped down to his chest; a mouth as keen and narrow as a knife-blade; a forehead made even loftier by the recession of his crinkly grey hair. He wore a midnight-blue mohair suit, with black shoes and tie, and was so allover immaculate that Blake felt like having him gift-wrapped and sent home as a present.

'If you have quite finished examining me, Mr—?'

'Smith.'

'Such a name could only be your own. Unless you are trying to mock me at this early stage in the charade.'

'Charade?'

'Sport, guessing-game, bluff. Only the names are different.'

His voice also was appropriate. Tight, high-pitched, tinny.

Blake shifted feet. 'You read the form I completed. You've presumably studied the . . . specimen I sent up. I think you know what I'm here for.'

Petersen nodded and stalked to his desk. He sat down

behind it in a massive satin-chrome and black leather chair. The seat of the chair must have been padded for he remained respectably in sight, his head level with the photograph of Karen and her mother.

'You want to see me about some allegedly "missing property",' he said bluntly. 'What missing property would that be? I have lost nothing. My company has lost nothing. This office you are standing in has lost nothing. Look around you, Mr Smith.' He paused and levelled a finger like a manicured claw at a picture of yellow wheatfields, green mountains and blue sea. 'My Brian Bradshaw is still on the wall, and there is nothing else of intrinsic value worth taking. As for my home, you and a band of mercenaries would have difficulty in storming it. You are bluffing. You have nothing of mine, and never will have.'

'Before I answer, do you mind if I take a seat?'

'Be my guest.' He waved Blake into a steel-and-leather chair, ugly and uncomfortable enough to be the product of a design centre.

'I may have nothing personal belonging to you,' said Blake, erasing Karen from his mind. 'But I do have access to three million pounds-worth of missing diamonds which were insured by your company.'

'I know of no—'

'They were "lost" somewhere between Johannesburg and London two weeks ago. You should read *The Cape Times*. The theft made the front page three days running.'

Petersen inclined his head. 'I read about the incident. But what makes you think—'

Again Blake interrupted him. 'I *know* they were insured by you, and I also know that at this very moment you are processing the cheque which will eventually be paid to your clients. The combine I represent has inside information about your company, Mr Petersen. Information that, from such a source as theirs, cannot be queried or faulted.'

'Hey, man! You are talking about a leak? Here in Cape Town?'

'Possibly. Or it could be in Jo'burg, or Durban, or Glasgow, or London. Anywhere you have offices, the organization I work for has . . . contacts.'

'So well-hidden there is no point in my seeking them out?'

'Your investigators are welcome to try. But they'll have to start right at the top. With you.'

'So, Mr Smith, you consider me a cornered, if not beaten, man? Ready to comply with your every demand.'

'I haven't made any yet.'

'No. But *I* would in your place. If only on the strength of this piece of . . . hexagonal quartz.'

He unclenched his left hand and rolled the diamond across the leather top of the table. It boggled like a rock arriving at the foot of a mountain. Turned over for a last time and lay still.

'You know as well as I do,' Blake said, 'that it's not quartz. If it had been I wouldn't have got past the lobby.'

'As I said – a cornered man.'

'Ready to discuss terms.'

'Ready to *listen* to them.'

'They really are very simple,' Blake added, then stopped as Petersen's hand slid beneath the desk, opened an out-of-sight drawer.

'Worry not,' he said smiling. 'I am not activating a tape-recorder.'

'Because one has been playing ever since I entered the room.'

He shrugged apologetically.

'One has to keep records. Company records.'

Blake looked on as Petersen closed the drawer and displayed what he had taken from it. A toy. A plastic figure of a chocolate-coloured monkey dressed in a white waistcoat with black buttons; a brown collarless suit; a red, green and yellow bow-tie. In each paw it held a drumstick, and the drum itself was fitted into a slot under its silver-buckled belt. A length of green flex was connected to the creature's bottom; a long unnatural tail ending in a green rubber bulb which, as Petersen pressed it, made the monkey beat monotonously on the instrument.

'Don't alarm yourself,' he remarked. 'It is not in any way symbolic.'

'Then *what* is it?'

'Some people take to drink, some to drugs, others fool with worry-beads. Personally I find it more soothing to play the timpano, by proxy.'

For a few slow seconds Blake listened to the noise the toy made. Hailstones striking a corrugated iron roof.

'If you feel like continuing,' prompted Petersen. 'The terms. Remember?'

'You must accept that I had nothing to do with the . . . removal of the stones,' Blake declared. 'I don't know exactly when they were stolen, or how. I don't even know their present whereabouts – with the exception of that sample there.'

The pitch of the drum increased. Tap-tap-tap-tap-tap-tap-tap.

'Naturally not,' Petersen agreed. 'You are no more than an agent, a middleman, someone out to do both parties concerned a service.'

'That's how I see it.'

'Then, as a dutiful middleman, you must tell me how much my company is to pay for the return of the stones.'

Blake answered quickly. 'Less than three million pounds.'

A further salvo on the drums.

'It would need to be. Otherwise how would I benefit from the proposed deal?'

'By getting the jewels back, your company's reputation would become doubly secure. Besides, exchanges of this nature are by no means uncommon or unethical. I'm sure your shareholders would approve.'

'Doubtless.'

'I could insist on receiving the full market value, and you would be loath not to agree.'

Tap-tip-tap-tip-tap-tip.

'Try me and see.'

'My instructions are not to do that. I am only to ask for—' He hesitated. 'A straight two million. No more, no less, no haggling.'

Tip-tip-tip-tip.

'Rand or sterling?'

'Pounds sterling.'

'To be paid how? In kind? Cash? Bonds? An open cheque?'

'A certified draft paid into a bank of my nomination.'

'Here in Cape Town?'

Blake shook his head.

'Geneva.'

The rhythm changed – became more feverish and intense.

'A numbered account!' he uttered.

'Naturally.'

'Very professional of you, Mr, er?' He snapped his fingers.

'Still Smith.'

'Professional and knowledgable. You have done this sort of work before?'

'Acted as go-between? Several times.'

'And always with success.'

'First time, last time, this time.'

'And the next.'

'That too.'

The drum sounded a sad tattoo; a signal of defeat, recalling the troops to barracks.

'You are fortunate to be dealing in diamonds,' Petersen said as he released the rubber bulb, put the monkey back in its drawer.

'In what way?'

He stood and steered Blake to the door.

'The very rarity of the stones makes them a commodity more valuable and negotiable than gold. Since mining began only eighty tons of the mineral have been produced. Although the gems are now being found in a variety of unlikely places. Russia and the Sahara, to name but two.'

'How fascinating.'

'Indeed it is. But not as fascinating as the meeting I shall convene once you have gone.'

'Meeting?'

'Don't sound so alarmed. My meeting will not be with the police – you know, of course, that I cannot go to them. No, this will be here in this room with my fellow-directors. I may be what the natives call the *baas*, but I still have to consult with my colleagues where two million rand is concerned.'

'Pounds.'

'But of course.'

Petersen paused and put a hand on Blake's wrist. It felt as if a scrawny bird had alighted there.

'One last question, Mr Smith.'

'Yes?'

'May I know what percentage you are receiving for your services.'

'Five.'

'I don't suppose an increase of five would tempt you to change sides?'

'No, it wouldn't. I told you, I know nothing about names, identities, addresses, or whereabouts. My contact is a man called Jones. He rings me when he needs to use me. I don't ring him because I don't have his number.'

'Fair enough, Mr Smith. Telephone me at this time on Monday and I will let you know our decision, and what, if any, the arrangements are.'

'Will do.'

'And Mr Smith – there is a saying about diamonds. That as long as women are born and men fall in love, there will always be a demand for them. I would now like to add a rider to that.'

Blake looked at Petersen attentively.

'That as long as crooks are made and businessmen forced to deal with them, the demand will become an obsession. Not for justice, but for retribution and revenge. Do I get through to you?'

'All the way.'

'Good. Then I too have succeeded.'

CHAPTER FORTY-FOUR

As the door closed on Blake, another one opened at the back of Petersen's office. Softly, silently, as if the person behind it was unsure of his reception. When the man with the hearing-aid entered, however, it was with the confident poise of a winner. He waited until Petersen had returned to his desk, sat spinning on the black chair in lazy half-circles. Then he came forward, the light striking sparks off his purple silk suit.

'You've got to grant him one thing,' he said, stopping at the desk and giving a short-lipped smile.

'Bravado?' hazarded Petersen.

'That and expertise. For a beginner he knows how to

swing a job. I couldn't have bettered his approach work myself.'

'A real compliment.'

'I mean it. Blake's got style. Another man would have taken that infernal monkey of yours and—'

Petersen stilled his chair. 'He overreached himself,' he interrupted contemptuously. 'Just as you were in danger of doing.'

'Me?'

'Don't think I haven't had reservations about this intrigue. There were several times when I was close to calling it off.'

'Then why didn't you?'

'Curiosity. I was curious to see which of you was the craftier. If you'd failed I'd have been just as ruthless towards you as I now shall be to Blake.'

'And the money and your daughter. Don't they count?'

'Naturally. But Karen I'd already lost. And the money could possibly be deducted against tax. Despite what you and Blake may think, they were the least of my considerations.'

'So what was the most?'

'The fun of it. This has given me more kicks than making my first million ever did. And once you have that first elusive million, the others follow automatically.'

The man with the hearing-aid smiled.

'Pleased to have pleased you.'

'Don't mention it. You took all the risks—'

'Calculated ones.'

'— and I shall reap the dividend.'

'We'll both do that, Theo.'

'I can't make decisions for Karen – you should know that.'

'But you can influence her.'

'A slight nudge, no more.'

'Then the intrigue continues.'

'A tip-off to the police?'

'Nothing too definite. Just enough to pressure Blake into playing things our way. Within three months I'll return both your properties to you. I'll have my informant contact Scotland Yard and then I shall personally *cherchez la femme*.'

Petersen held his hands in front of his face.

'Hey – don't spoil it for me!'

'It's flattering to have your confidence.'

Petersen lowered his hands.

'You've always had that. I'd lay money on you to out-think and outmanoeuvre Blake.'

'Why?'

'Because you'd always put yourself in his place. Ask yourself, 'What would *I* do now?" Try and sell the diamonds for peanuts and risk betrayal and arrest? Or make a deal with White Star? In a way, he only does as you will him. There's only one thing I don't, and never will, understand.'

'Yes?'

'How Karen ever got involved with two such *skelms*!'

CHAPTER FORTY-FIVE

Blake was reassured by the threat contained in Petersen's last few sentences. Up until then the interview had been too smooth and too gentlemanly. He felt he could deal with intimidation and outspoken menace; it was the man whose grip was firm, whose eyes twinkled, whose voice never lost its blandness that he was wary of. Even so, on leaving the building he went to great lengths to shake-off any possible pursuer.

His progress around the city, from the Botanical Gardens to the castle, convinced him that he was not being shadowed. As an added precaution he sauntered down the oak-lined pedestrians-only stretch of Government Avenue, and went into Cartwright's Corner House, on the junction of Adderley and Darling Streets. He walked to the toy centre on the first floor, and bought a plush teddy-bear and a painted wooden engine for the boys.

It was after lunchtime when he finally got back to the hotel. The hall porter told him his family had already eaten and gone to their room. He ran upstairs and led the boys onto the balcony, where they played with their gifts beneath a poppy-red sunblind. Then he and Karen retired to the bedroom. He stood mutely while she lolled on the spread with her feet tucked under her.

'Well,' she said impatiently, 'don't go all coy on me. What did you think of him and how did it go?'

He stood by the window, looking out at the incongruous minaret of a mosque.

'Do you mean his appearance?' he hedged. 'Or the man behind it?'

'We all know he looks like an undeveloped freak. I'd like your estimate of his character.'

'In three words. Tough; fly; and ruthless.'

'An unholy trinity.'

'You should be telling me.'

'Why undermine your confidence?'

'He went for the deal anyway. Or at least he pretended to. He didn't have a feasible alternative.'

'What exactly did he say?'

'That he'd put my proposition before his board of directors. He has the say-so, but they also have a voice.'

'United or dis—?'

'They're bound to tear each other's throats. No company is going to hand over two million quid just like that.'

'Two *million*!'

'Not a decimal penny less.'

'I don't know whether to laugh, cry, or have the full nervous breakdown.'

'You and me both.'

'It just doesn't seem possible, Phil. That you – we – are holding him to ransom for two million pounds!'

'I knew what I was doing.'

'*Did* you, Phil? Did you *really*?'

'The side effects are also beneficial.'

'In what way?'

'They've brought us closer together than we have been in years. We're a unit, a pair.'

'Being close to someone is not the same, or as desirable, as being deep.'

He frowned. 'I'm sorry, darling, I'm not with you.'

'What I mean is we're clutching at each other on the surface like survivors clinging to a raft. But underneath, where it really counts, we're drifting apart.'

'Not that *I'm* aware of.'

'That's the trouble. You *wouldn't* be! It takes a woman to see what is actually happening, and not just what appears to be!'

She saw him go rigid.

'How much longer will it take, Phil?' she asked softly.

'I'm contacting your father again on Monday. After that, if he confirms the exchange, I'll fly to Geneva and organize the bank. You don't open a numbered account by postcard.'

'What happens to the boys and I in the meantime?'

'You stay put.'

Decisively, she shook her head.

'We can't stay here.'

'Why not? It's inconspicuous.'

'Not enough so. I took the boys out shopping this morning and saw someone I used to know.'

'On the street?'

'In a boutique fifty yards away. A girl I was friendly with at university. She acts as though she's the owner. We'll have to move out. And today.'

'Any idea where?'

'It's off-season and we can rent a bungalow at Clifton – that's a suburb about five miles from here. Beautiful white sandy beaches – even more beautiful "bikini girls" in the summer – and little chance of my being recognized.'

'You're sure of that?'

'Positive. Clifton's on the Atlantic coast. At this time of year with the Cape winds still blowing it'll be relatively deserted. And there are other blessings.'

'Such as?'

'The sunsets.'

'*Sunsets!*'

'Each night the sun drowns there in the sea. It's very—'

'Spare me the travelogue. It's "beautiful".'

'But it *is*!'

CHAPTER FORTY-SIX

The bungalow they rented at Clifton, on the slopes below Lion's Head, was hardly the 'dream palace' he had planned for Karen. Its predominant features were the vast burglar alarms on the doors and windows – black and ugly, like the kind seen outside old warehouses. The only resemblance it had to the home he'd visualized was that it was on the side of a hill. It would have taken the talents of the wiliest estate agent to make something of its stark, packing-case shape, low red-bricked roof, scanty *stoep*, and the two jacaranda trees that stood like pensioned-off retainers on either side of the cast-iron gate. He apologized for it to Karen, but she cut him off saying:

'It's only temporary so why grieve?'

'No reason, only—'

'You don't have to buy me. I came free of charge a long while back.'

'That doesn't mean you should be underprivileged.'

'Because there isn't a turbo-grill barbecue, or white bentwood coat stands?'

'Most women would appreciate such luxuries.'

'I would also appreciate a husband with roots and permanence. A name that was really my own and not a cover-up. A sense of stability.'

'They'll come.'

'So will lots of things.'

'Like death and taxes.'

She laughed jaggedly.

'In your case, Phil, you can only count on the first.'

So it went, their first weekend in 'Apostles' Rest'. The cottage took its name from the spiked mountain range, the Twelve Apostles, which formed the background to Clifton and its four beaches and clustered homes. The district was as beautiful as he'd been told, and Blake got enjoyment from watching the boys playing football on the tender white sand; kicking up froths of spray from the ocean;

running and turning somersaults among the umbrellas that were beginning to sprout like multi-coloured mushrooms.

Still he was aware of Karen's unpredictability and edginess. He knew he could keep her only by striking a balance between money and the security it could buy; and her concept of him as someone who had defied her father, so proving himself worthy of her admiration and respect.

On Sunday they ate their lunch on the *stoep*, and looked down on the men and girls lying like brown burns on the face of the beach. The bungalows and apartment buildings around them were starting to fill up with families similar to their own, and without Karen saying anything he realized that was what she wanted: to belong to and yet not be a part of.

After their biscuits and coffee the boys became bored and restless.

'Daddy,' said Ian in his smallest, most wheedling voice. 'Please may you take us to see grandad? *Please!*'

Prepared for this request, Blake said Petersen was in America on business.

'Then what can we *did*?'

'You can did this,' he replied, handing out a fistful of cents. 'Go and buy some "wice-cream" at the shop by the rocks. And don't either of you come back till you've eaten it all.'

Smiling together, Karen and he watched them race off – their feet touching the ground only now and then, the way seven-league boots do.

'That was a good question of Ian's', she said presently. 'About his grandfather.'

'I answered it convincingly.'

'It's easy to lie to a child.'

'So I told a fib. It's—'

'Not to Ian. To yourself. You're lying to yourself without even knowing you're doing it.'

'About what?'

'About *who*?'

'Name me a name.'

'Theo J. Petersen.'

'How am I lying about him?'

'By accepting your own ignorance of him. Did you know

that he's a *dopper*, a Calvinistic Afrikaner, and that he was born in Potchefstroom – which is as sin-conscious and guilt-ridden as Sodom and Gomorrah combined?'

'So?'

'So Potchefstroom is also the birthplace of the Broederbond, of which he is an implacable member.'

'Broederbond?'

'You've heard of the Freemasons and the Ku Klux Klan? Well, as secret societies go, it is positioned midway between the two. Less cosy and palsy-walsy than the first. Less ruthless and vicious than the second.'

'I don't see how—'

'It affects you,' she cut in, 'because it's not just my father and his company you're up against.'

'It's the Broederbond.'

'As long as you know it.'

Blake smiled sarcastically.

'You're asking me to believe that the entire membership of this Broederbond is going to gang up with your father and persecute and wreak vengeance on me?'

'Not all five thousand of them. But his cell will.'

'Cell?'

'The Broederbond is based on the cell system. They consist of from five to ten members. It's all very tight-knit and incestuous.'

'So the most I have to worry about is Petersen and a few of his secret society mates.'

'That's more than enough.'

'For me?'

'For you and an army.'

On the Monday morning they were awakened early by Ian stomping into the big front bedroom doing his monster-from-outer-space act. With eyes closed and arms held rigidly outwards, he stifflegged it around the room chanting: 'I-am-a-Dalek. You-must-be-ex-term-in-at-ed!' After a few moments spent crashing into the furniture, he reverted to being an Earthling. He sprinted to the draped window shouting, 'Shall I wake the curtains up, daddy?'

At breakfast the boys munched rapidly through their egg fluffs, and left the cottage to explode in the pebbled garden. Blake kissed Karen goodbye and took the A1 bus from Clifton to the terminus near Kottlers Curio Shop in Adderley Street. He then slotted five cents in a public call box to buy three minutes of Petersen's time.

The secretary – her voice as stereotyped as her appearance – put Blake straight through. There was a click as though someone had picked up an extension, and then Petersen spoke. He sounded even squeakier over the 'phone.

'My board and I have considered your proposal, Mr Smith,' he announced, 'and we have decided, in outline at least, to agree to your terms. There are several factors which still need to be clarified, but I see no reason why we should not have ourselves a deal.'

'Fine,' Blake replied. 'That only leaves when we meet and where.'

'The sooner the better. And where else but here?'

'I agree with the sooner. But not at your office. May I suggest a more neutral venue?'

'Please do.'

'How about a spot of culture? Something fine and artistic.'

'Ach, man! Stop acting like a spy!'

'A little tea-time self-improvement – say around five.'

'Where?'

'How does Frans Hals grab you?'

CHAPTER FORTY-SEVEN

It was getting on for five when Blake, as slow-paced and casual as any tourist, sauntered along Adderley Street and turned off into Greenmarket Square – where the Old Town House was situated. Originally built as quarters for the Town Guard, it now contained the Michaelis Collection of 17th century Dutch and Flemish paintings, of which Frans Hals' *Portrait of a Woman* was the most prestigious item. Blake had learned this – and received his inspiration – from a guidebook to the city. But he considered that, as a near native of the place, Petersen would have twigged his reference to the artist. Since ringing the businessman,

Blake had spent the day constructively, securing the three things which were essential if Karen and he were to stay together.

First of all he booked a return flight to Geneva, via Johannesburg and Zurich, leaving D. F. Malan Airport the following afternoon. Then with the dwindling remains of his money, he opened an account in the name of Howard Martin at a branch of the Standard Bank. He explained to the manager that his wife and he had 'fallen in love' with South Africa, and planned to settle there permanently.

'We have offices throughout the Republic and South West Africa,' the manager stated. 'You may enjoy cheque encashment facilities wherever it is you make your home.'

His final move was to buy a car. Part of Bart's legacy was an international driving licence – all the authority needed to get anything from a mini to a Rolls. The sort of job he had in mind would be fast, solid, spacious and not over-conspicuous. Resisting the appeal of a Bentley he settled for an imported Mercedes; the 300 SEL 6.3 model, with a top speed of 137 miles per hour.

The manager of the car showroom agreed to take a post-dated cheque, said he would have the saloon serviced and ready to drive away the moment the cheque was cleared. Blake told him it should be no later than Saturday, left to eat a late salad lunch and keep his appointment with Petersen. He was nervous, as tightly wound as the insides of a golfball. The sensation heightened as he crossed the square and regarded the house with its balcony from which government proclamations had been read, the small-paned windows and the little domed tower, as absurd and frivolous as a spring hat, which had once held a gong used to summon the burghers.

A squad of students and sightseers loitered in front of the building as if waiting for comfort or alms. Blake picked his way through them and paid his ten cents' admission money. Inside, the house was a replica of the Dutch interiors of the period. Immediately he was possessed by the death-in-a-vacuum feeling that came to him in museums, galleries or waxworks. He had chosen the rendezvous with care, selecting the kind of atmosphere and surroundings in which Petersen could not easily trap or surprise him. There could be no assaults or beatings-up in such a place;

once outside it there were half-a-dozen escape routes he could take if he had to.

The pictures, as such, did not interest him and he walked slack-eyed past the Rembrandt etchings, the Steens, the van Goyens, the Cuyps and the van Beyerens. He only paused when he came to the Hals and sat on a rest bench facing the picture. He knew nothing about painting and couldn't tell whether the work was of genius or not. But there was something about the woman herself with her crossed hands, bold 'seeing' eyes and irregular mouth that reached out to him. Perhaps it was the slight suggestion of a smile, the way the hair was drawn back to emphasize the forehead, that gave her an appearance of . . . astuteness, a person not to be kidded or fooled.

Forgetting the time, his reason for being there almost, he tried to outstare her. An ache penetrated his forehead, punched at the bone and tissue like a fist trying to get out. His eyes felt tired, smarted as if he had gazed too long into an open fire. He shook his head, gave the woman best in the contest, massaged the skin around his temples.

Suddenly, a shadow spliced the bench. He looked up and saw Petersen staring down at him, his lips concealed by a tight smile.

'Have I kept you waiting?' he asked mockingly. 'Or are you practising meditation?'

He sat next to Blake, crossed his legs and gazed quizzically at the picture.

'Sorry. I was just—'

'Daydreaming of riches – hard to come by, harder still to account for.'

'I'm only the middleman, remember. It's my clients who'll have that problem.'

'How forgetful of me.'

'How crude!'

'Really, Mr Smith, I'm in no way trying to—'

'Trick me? You'll have to be a bloody sight smarter than that!'

Petersen shook his head and tut-tutted.

'You must guard against nerves. Already I can see cracks in your make-up. More even than the *Woman* looking so superciliously upon us.'

A party of schoolchildren sloped by, press-ganged into culture.

Blake stoppered his temper.

'Save your concern.'

'Certainly.'

'Just talk business.'

'I take it we can converse openly here. Or would you prefer somewhere more secluded – free from the artlovers of the world?'

'Right here is fine. The bench isn't bugged, and no one can jump us.'

'Hey – don't you trust me?'

'But for your sarcasm, you appear to be unarmed.'

'You know, Mr Smith,' said Petersen sadly, 'in other circumstances I could get to appreciate you. Not actually like you. But certainly have you on my team. If you can't beat them, buy them.'

'I'm not for sale.'

'At any price?'

'Under two million pounds.'

'My advisers tell me that twenty-five percent is the usual rate payable on exchange deals. Are you greedy, Mr Smith? Or have you only partly revealed your hand?'

'The combine who employ me make the terms – not me.'

'But such extravagant ones.'

'They proposition from strength.'

'In what way?'

'As I told you earlier, they have inroads into your company. Not just here, but in all your branches at home and abroad. If you fail to please them they will hit you again where it hurts.'

'And where might that be?'

'In your public image.'

'Mine, or White Star's?'

'Does it matter?'

'They are one and the same.'

'Then may I proceed?'

Like Petersen, Blake raised his eyes to the *Woman*; it seemed as if they were addressing each other through her.

'I'm instructed to tell you,' he stated, 'that the stones will be returned to you in the following manner; that and no other. If you are going to disagree, do so now and I can terminate the negotiations. We shall not meet again afterwards, and no further contact will be made.'

'I'm listening.'

'You will today – and without delay – send the necessary draft to a nominated bank in Geneva. As soon as the bank has received it, the diamonds will also be put in their charge. Once that has been done, the exchange will be performed by the bank's director. He will credit the draft to the payee, and return the stones to you. It is simple, straightforward and—'

'Honest.'

'Free from double-cross.'

'And the name of the bank?'

'The Vattel Bank in the Rue des Granges.'

'It is not one of the big banks?'

'One of the "privates".'

As they finished talking, a uniformed attendant entered the room, announced that it was 5.30 and the gallery was closing. Blake and Petersen stood up – waited while the schoolchildren were shunted past them by a master haggard with responsibility.

Petersen smiled, still looking at the picture.

'Are you married, Mr Smith?' he asked pleasantly.

'Yes,' replied Blake unthinkingly.

'So was Frans Hals. A wife and ten hungry children. He had so many debts that a baker to whom he owed money forced him into bankruptcy. At the time of his examination in Haarlem he owned three mattresses and bolsters, a wardrobe and five pictures. Nothing more in the world.'

'I don't see—'

'It has everything to do with you. Hals was a master, but that didn't stop his wife and he being sent to the poorhouse. He was destitute in his last years and dependent on charity. In a way, of course, he was more fortunate than you will be. The burghers took pity on him and he was granted an annuity of two hundred florins a year.'

Blake's body twitched. He approached Petersen, hands knotted.

'Don't bother to come out with me. I know the way. I only hope you know yours.'

He nodded to Blake, turned and walked crisply from him. The audience was over.

CHAPTER FORTY-EIGHT

Karen, when he told her his plans, took them as calmly as if he'd proposed a day's outing to the country. She was so steady and self-composed that he suspected she was glad to be free of him for a while. Only the boys showed their disappointment; Alastair in particular sulked because he couldn't go along. Blake tempered his dejection by playing football on the beach until the light drained from the sky, and there was nothing left of the sun but a damp red stain on the ocean. As they scuffed back to the cottage Alastair asked if he could see his father off at the airport.

'Go on, Dad,' he pleaded. 'I've never been to an airfield before.'

'I don't know if your mother—'

'Mum can come too. And Ian.'

'Well, if it's all right with her—'

'Thanks, Dad! I'll run and ask her.'

He ploughed off through the sand, leaving Blake to carry the black-and-white football with 'World Cup 1974' stamped upon it. The youngster had completed his sales talk when Blake reached Apostles' Rest, and he was glad to see Karen flushed and beaming.

'Sounds a fun idea,' she said. 'You always promised to take them to Heathrow and never did.'

'It'll give you something to do with them. They'll be a handful all day long when I'm away.'

She nodded. 'I don't want to go on the beach too much in case someone should recognize me. But I can hardly cringe in the house while they're up to their necks in seawater.'

'Why not hire a nanny?'

'Bit grand, isn't it?'

'A girl, then, to look after them. There's bound to be a domestic agency in Cape Town. You pay her by the day and she enjoys herself as much as they do.'

'I might just do that.'

'I'd feel a lot easier if you did.'

He followed her through to the kitchen. And, as the boys played tag in the garden, gave a synopsis of his conversation with her father. She smiled bleakly when he'd finished, belaboured the steak she was preparing.

'Sounds just like him. Polite and tricky, meek and deceitful. Only the gimmick with the monkey is new. Before that he chewed his nails.'

'I hope I haven't underestimated him.'

'Whatever you think of him is not enough – for good or bad. He's better than he allows you to believe, and worse than he lets you know. Another thing. Who left who at the gallery?'

'He went first to get the draft off. I followed on with the visitors.'

'So he had a start on you.'

'What difference does it make? It's the bank that has the power now.'

'Give him an inch and you're a mile behind him. Give him a minute and you're an hour astray.'

'I'll take care.'

'Then we've nothing to worry about – have we?'

The next morning Blake did something he'd never done before to the boys. He deliberately went back on a promise to them. Despite their tears and tantrums, he told them that he wouldn't be taking them to the airport after all. He'd slept badly that night, tormented by dreams which went by like telegraph poles seen from a racing train but which were none the less ominous and dreadfilled. When he wasn't dreaming, he lay awake lathered in sweat, listening to every sound made by the darkened room; each squeak, sigh and tick. His nerves were rubbed naked by breakfast-time, and he needed to be alone.

'That's the meanest thing I've ever seen,' cried Karen, as the boys fled bawling from the room.

'With a father like yours I find that hard to believe!'

'He was many things I despised. But never a liar!'

'Nobody's lying! I just don't think it's wise.'

'It's not wisdom they need. It's truth and honesty.'

'Don't I give them that already? And love.'

'Alastair and Ian are no more than appendages to you!

You don't treat them as people in their own right. They're pieces pushed about on that criminal chessboard you have for a mind. Pawns to be sacrificed to your greed and ambitions. Then, when you've lost them, you'll have to give up the queen. When you do that, you'll be on your own again, Philip!'

He started to defend himself, but she turned and hurried to the *stoep*, where the boys were using the side of the cottage as a wailing wall. Later, as he collected his grip, he listened numbly to her grievances.

'It's a coward's time to go – with the children upset and me beginning a period. Or is that part of your strategy, too?'

'Contact the agency like I mentioned. They'll send someone round to help you.'

'And if they don't?'

'I'll be back by the weekend. Surely you can cope until then.

'I'll have to, won't I?'

'So don't bloody well bitch!'

On reaching the city he went to the hotel he had stayed at earlier and spent the next few hours anaesthetizing himself in the bar. Once again he carried the diamonds loose in his pockets. He reckoned that no-one at the airport – in Cape Town or Geneva – would bother to search a drunk. He felt the brandies scalding his stomach as he left the hotel and lumbered to the Airways Terminal at the foot of Adderley Street. It was a long time since he'd been so cut, and he wondered how he could exist again sober.

CHAPTER FORTY-NINE

He stayed drunk most of the next day, too, and saw Geneva wobble and shift before him. He decided against staying in one of the luxury hotels like the Beau Rivage or the Richemond, and chose an unpretentious *pension* in La place du Bourg-de-Four. The tiny square was overshadowed by the green spire of St Peter's Cathedral, which he used as a lodestar on his tour that night of the city's bars and dives.

He remembered ordering grilled fish and a bottle of

Pouilly Fuissé in a restaurant by the lake. But after that – nothing. He imagined a cab must have taken him to the *pension*, and he probably made another fool of himself there. It seemed so the next morning, from the way the manageress avoided him, the waitresses giggled, the hunch-backed porter grinned as he went to keep his appointment at the bank.

'It's a good morning, sir,' the porter said as Blake shielded his eyes from the sunlight. 'You can see Mont Blanc today. That is a good omen. It will bring you luck.'

'Thanks,' Blake said, thrusting a five-franc piece into his palm. 'I'm going to need it.'

The Vattel Bank had been Bart's idea. He'd explained about the Swiss banking system – how it was structured in seven classes, from the large Cantonal banks, to the small "privates", which were not allowed to advertise for deposits, and were not legally required to publish their balance sheets. There were some sixty of these *banquiers*; each one listed in the 'phone book, and each one sheltered behind aspic-like facades which had been unchanged for decades.

At the time Blake thought the accountant was merely trying to impress him. But as he entered the Rue des Granges he got an inkling of what Bart had meant. Unlike the Avenue de la Republiqué, where most of the major banks were located, the street was prudently without glass-and-bronze front doors, halls with marble pilasters, leather armchairs and sombre paintings. The houses were set away from the pavement and could have been the mansions of the Protestant bankers who had started operations there in the eighteenth century.

The bank to which he had cabled and received a reply hid behind an ivy-shrouded garden wall, with an elaborate iron gate opening onto a gravel drive. The only indication that it *was* a bank came from a plaque tucked among the ivy – two words in sloping bas relief: Vattel Bank. Blake pushed back the gate, crunched up to the polished oak door, and pressed a lozenge-shaped bell in the woodwork. A short wait and the door was opened by a weedy, sallow-faced youth who could have stood behind any shop counter. Blake told him his business was private, exclusively with Monsieur Vattel. The youth nodded, showed him to a fragile, gilt chair opposite a solarium and disappeared into one of the dim adjoining rooms.

Somewhere at the rear of the house a clock struck eleven. Blake counted each stroke, was still listening to the reverberation when the office door reopened and the young man beckoned him inside. He silently withdrew and Blake walked towards a red-topped Empire desk, behind which sat a thin, neat, elderly man with a grey-streaked goatee beard. The man stood as Blake approached and offered him his hand.

'I'm delighted to meet you, Mr Martin,' he said in a low, considerate voice. 'And more delighted to place the facilities of my bank at your disposal.'

'Thank you,' Blake said, taking a chair at right-angles to him. 'I hope we will both benefit from our association.'

'Doubtless, doubtless. I have assisted several of your fellow-countrymen who wished to remove their heads from beneath the guillotine of taxation.'

'The Scarlet Pimpernel of finance.'

'Indeed.'

His withered hands fumbled across the desk, sought the letter Blake had sent him from Las Palmas. He found it, held it up as though appraising the watermark, read it through a *pince-nez*.

'You state here,' he said finally, 'that you wish me to act as administrator to the trade proposed between yourself and Mr Petersen. That is Mr Theo J. Petersen, of Cape Town.'

'That's correct. Have you heard from him yet?'

The banker again shuffled his papers.

'This arrived this morning.' He flourished a sheet of yellow paper. 'It authorizes me to credit two million pounds in an account for you. In exchange for this, you will provide me with some . . . collateral.'

'I have it right here,' Blake replied, putting the suede purse before him. 'You'd better check to make sure the goods are complete.'

'You'll forgive me if I have your collateral evaluated? It is not that I don't trust you. But when the stakes are this high, the cards must be examined.'

He touched a bell on the underside of the desk. The youth

re-entered and flitted across the floor. He mutely took the purse and skated back to the door.

'As quick as you can, Jean-Louis,' said the broker. 'Mr Martin is a busy man.'

But Blake was already on his feet. Before he could speak the banker added: 'However it is better that the gems do not leave our sight. I can test them myself first.' The assistant returned, handed back the purse. Vattel opened it, took a small file from his pocket, and prodded each jewel in turn. 'This is all that is required,' he said quietly. 'If they were made of paste they would have a low degree of hardness and would yield to the file. It will be necessary, however, for Jean-Louis to ascertain whether or not they are glass.' This time the youth took the diamonds to a table by the window, examined them beneath an ebony microscope. Vattel smiled at Blake's curiosity and said, 'Glass was made in Egypt as early as 1600 BC, and imitation gems date from the same period.'

'What shows the difference?'

'Under the microscope glass reveals the unnatural nature of its formation caused by the comparatively rapid cooling. Also there are fissures, cracks and small star-like markings due to a kind of . . . premature decomposition. As for synthetic stones – they show their origin by colour bands and gas bubbles along the curved edges.'

'So the crooked cannot win.'

'In Switzerland we acknowledge only one kind of crook. He who steals from banks.'

Blake sat down again, was made uncomfortable by the banker's stare. Vattel seemed about to say something, hesitated, then changed his mind. He rose and moved to a half-moon drinks' cabinet set against the red velour wall.

'Absinthe or sherry, Mr Martin?'

'Sherry. Dry.'

'You'll forgive me if I choose absinthe for myself? Like suicide, it is the vice of the banking fraternity.'

'Suicide?'

'Indeed yes.' He passed Blake the drink and returned to his seat. 'Absinthe can destroy the mind, and with it the man. I allow myself a glass a morning – no more and no less. The Swiss banker is so highly disciplined, he must have a weakness – or crack. Despite our enviable peace and prosperity, we have one of the highest suicide rates in the world.'

'The pressures must be great.'

'They are. And understandably so. Ever since our private accounts were first 'exposed' in the early 'thirties by a Gestapo agent, Georg Thomae, we have been threatened with jail sentences if we disclose the existence of an account without the depositor's permission. Thomae was sent here by Hitler to discover which Germans were sending money out of the country. By means of bribery, he succeeded in this and so brought about the Banking Code of 1934.'

'Which guarantees me total anonymity.'

'Outside of the bank, yes. Inside, your identity will be known only to myself and my Director of Numbered Accounts. And *we* shall not betray you.'

'No matter how my money was obtained?'

'Your morals are no concern of ours, Mr Martin. We do not create crime, and the money we receive is not just hoarded. It is put to work by us to benefit the general economy. Is there any difference, I ask you, between accepting deposits from the Mafia and the CIA? Money only smells when you don't have it, Mr Martin. And the smell it gives off is a sweet and seductive perfume. One that any man – or woman – would give his birthright to wear.'

Blake was spared answering him by the completion of the assistant's work. The youth put the bag reverentially back on the table, bowed, and left. Blake looked at Vattel and the banker spread open his hands.

'Consider yourself my client.'

Ten minutes later Blake ground his way down the gravel drive. His head was bloated with facts about the numbered account he'd been accorded. All he had to do to draw money – up to forty thousand pounds, or its equivalent in foreign currency – was to write a sequence of letters and digits on the cheque form. The odds against anyone hitting on the code were several billion to one. No-one could open his bank box without a court order – which was almost impossible to obtain. His statements, and all correspondence, would be sent to him in plain brown envelopes. To deal with urgent queries a bank agent would visit him, at a time and place specified by himself.

He had nearly reached the gate when he heard someone hurrying behind him. He turned and saw Vattel's assistant hobbling up, a newspaper in his hand.

'Monsieur Vattel asked me to give you this,' he panted.

Blake took the paper – an airmail edition of *The Times* – from him. He unfolded the paper and examined the front page. A picture leapt up at him like an unleashed dog. It was of himself as Philip Blake – one of the mug-shots taken at Manston. Its resemblance to Howard Martin was more than just passing. Without the glasses, with his hair growing in again, the paraffin dissolving in his nose, he could pass for the brother of the man in the news. He forced his eyes onto the headline.

> Ex-Convict and Former Government
> Agent Sought for Heathrow
> Diamond Theft.

It was not that, however, that alarmed him. It was the byline below it.

From David Temple-Forbes
Cape Town, September 21.

CHAPTER FIFTY

The first thing he did on returning to the *pension* was put in a telephone call to Karen. He was told by the Geneva operator that there'd be a short delay, and he spent the time reading *The Times*' report in detail. Clancy, he learnt, had been arrested by the police the day before. Acting on 'information received', Detective-Inspector Dewhurst had gone to Southend where the 'wanted man' was arrested in a lodging-house in Western Esplanade. Before leaving with his prisoner for London, the officer said:

'That still leaves two of the gang at large. Arnold Monkton and Blake. We have leads as to the whereabouts of both men, and measures will be taken to effect their speedy arrests.'

The story ended with a late round-up of the situation. 'Last night Detective-Inspector Dewhurst set up a temporary crime headquarters in the Helmsley Motor Inn in

Cape Town's Hof Street. Blake is still believed to be here in the city, and early developments are expected.'

That was all, except for a three-line item at the foot of the page. The heading was: SECOND DIAMOND MAN CAUGHT. And the wording: Arnold Monkton, 47, one of the men sought in the Heathrow diamond robbery, was apprehended at midnight last night by police in County Monaghan, Ireland. Arrangements were being made to transfer him to London.'

Blake bunched up the paper and threw it across the room. Immediately, as if answering a signal, the telephone bleeped, and he eagerly lifted the receiver.

'Your call to Cape Town, sir,' said the operator. 'Your party is on the line now.'

There was a silence, and he shouted into the telephone.

'Hello, darling. Are you there?'

More silence.

'Karen. Can you hear me?'

'Mr Martin?'

The voice, a woman's, was so familiar that at first he thought it was Karen's.

'I'm afraid Mrs Martin cannot come to the phone, sir. She has asked me to take a message.'

'Who is this?'

'My name is Miss Gordimer. I was employed to look after your sons.'

'I'd like to speak to my wife, please. At once.'

'I'm sorry, sir. That's not possible.'

'Why not?'

'Mrs Martin is not well.'

'What's happened? She's not—'

'No, sir, it's nothing serious. But she's in bed, and is too weak to come to the telephone. She's lost a lot of blood.'

Blood. That gave him the clue. It was Karen's period. She was one of those women who suffered, who was cramped in agony each month. She would not be able to travel, to join him in Switzerland.

'Is there any message I can give to Mrs Martin?'

'It's personal.'

'Then it must wait your return.'

'Let me speak to one of the boys. To Alastair.'

'I'm sorry, sir, but Master Alastair is on the beach.'

'Ian then.'

'Master Ian too.'

His temper erupted.

'Shout for them to come in, God dammit!'

'That's not possible, sir. They're out of earshot.'

'Are you being deliberately bloody-minded? If you can't get my wife to the 'phone, then get the blasted 'phone to her! Failing that, go out and find Alastair and bring him to speak to me.'

'I have to go now, sir. Your wife needs attention.'

'Listen—'

'I shall tell Mrs Martin to expect you home soon.'

The receiver in Clifton crashed down, jarring his ear. He spoke to the operator, asked her to get the number back. There was a five-minute wait. Then she said blandly:

'I'm afraid there is no reply to Cape Town, sir.'

'There's another delay?'

'No, sir. The lines to South Africa are clear now. But your party no longer answers. Would you like me to keep the call in, sir, and try again later?'

He hung up without answering.

It was the evening of the following day when his 'plane touched down at D. F. Malan airport, in the city where he had vowed he would not risk his freedom again. In a way, Blake was glad that he had received the telephone call, that the girl had been so mysterious and curt. It showed him what he hadn't totally appreciated – that he cared for more than just loot and profit. His feelings for Karen and the boys had not – as he feared they might – been downgraded by greed and the desire to confound Petersen. Only a fool, he reckoned, or someone emotionally hooked, would chance what he was doing now. But somehow he didn't care if he was caught – it would only increase Karen's sympathy and loyalty. Make a hero figure of him, a rebel behind bars.

Thinking like this he strode nonchalantly through the terminal, challenging the stares of police and officials, daring them to stop him, search him, take him by the arm. But, despite the customs man who examined each page of his passport as if looking for a bribe, no one did so. He shrugged inwardly, took the airways bus to the Adderley Street Terminal, hired a cab to run him to Clifton. The driver was a talker, and conducted a one-way stream of dialogue out of the city centre and along Beach and Victoria Roads. He raised no more than a grunt from his passenger, who silently paid him and overtipped.

Blake waited until the taxi drove off, then he approached the cottage from the rear. The place seemed uninhabited, as though no-one had lived there since the previous summer. He cut through the overhanging bushes, scrambled along a path worn by children. As he did so, a light – yellow and watery – went on in the kitchen.

Cautiously, he made his way to the front *stoep*. There, as he crept up the steps, he heard the first sounds of life. The boys were arguing together in the living-room. Something about a missing roller skate. He halted by the half-open front door, with its rusted wire-netting and cracked panes of glass, peered into the unlit hall.

'Hello,' he called out. 'Is anyone there?'

The boys' dispute ceased abruptly, as though a radio had been switched off. He moved inside and headed towards the living-room. Suddenly the door to the kitchen opened and a girl – petite, slim, blonde – stood framed in the surrounds. He couldn't distinguish her face, but he'd seen her figure before.

'Miss Gordimer?' he hazarded.

'Yes, Mr Martin. I'm just making your wife's dinner.'

'She's feeling better?'

'A steady improvement.'

He edged nearer.

'Why were you so evasive on the 'phone?'

'I was only doing my job.'

'Which does not embrace hanging telephones up on me.'

'I was busy at the time.'

The second before he reached her she stepped back onto the checkered linoleum, one foot on a black square, the other on a white. She lifted her head and the light trickled weakly onto her face.

'Miss Van Heerden?' he queried. 'Denisē?'

The air stewardess smiled coldly.

'You're late,' she reprimanded. 'Boorishly late—'

'I got here as soon as I—'

'– for our date in London. You are several weeks overdue.'

He was going to say something. But as his mouth opened he was pincered from behind by two pairs of arms; a dry, dusty rag was forced between his teeth. Denise took a hypodermic syringe from the pocket of her starched white uniform. She held the syringe to the light and expertly depressed it. She stepped towards him with the needle poised.

'This won't take a moment,' she said. 'And it certainly won't hurt.'

One of the men holding him tugged up his sleeve. He had on a fawn Aertex sports shirt, his arm naked from the elbow down. He felt the needle pierce the skin – no more than a pinprick.

The derision on her face was the last thing he saw....

CHAPTER FIFTY-ONE

He didn't know how long he was unconscious, or semi-conscious. There were moments of waking, when he emerged from sleep like a diver surfacing from the seabed. Usually he found Denise bending over him, holding a hypodermic and jabbing it in his arm. It perhaps happened only two or three times; but it seemed like a score. He was aware of a drip attached to his other arm – the kind used in hospitals when the patient is too weak to eat anything – and of her saying 'You should have cut me in.'

At times she was joined by two men, the ones who had seized him. They were tall with their hair cut close to their scalps. They wore dark suits, white shirts, black ties and sunglasses. One of them – with the cleft chin and widow's peak – chewed gum all the time. The other smoked endless hand-rolled cigarettes which gave off a sharp, sweet, sickly smell.

Gradually, like a blind man regaining his eyesight, Blake itemized the room he was in. It had a domed ceiling, was high up (through the picture-window he could only see clouds and sky), and far more luxurious than anything in 'Apostles' Rest'. The decor had an aura of genteel sin; from the satinwood dressing-table and chairs, to the Dutch dolls which smirked saucily at him, perched on top of pouffes, wardrobes and occasional tables. He could hear the sea heave and sigh in the background, and once a light aeroplane flew low past the house, level with the window, so that he glimpsed its crimson wings and fuselage.

Soon after that he felt no more of the hypodermic. Denise stopped visiting him and the two bodyguards sat all day long at a table, playing pontoon and brag. They took turns to bring their meals on a tray so that he was never left alone. They seldom spoke to him unless it was to jeer.

Blake accepted the regime, asked them no questions, waited for their employer to show himself. He mostly slept in the hot afternoons and came-to one evening with the room warm, still, shadow bathed. The guards had gone and so had the card table. Without it, and with the curtains held back by velvet bows, the bedroom seemed more than ever like a mistress's boudoir. He yawned and stretched experimentally. First his legs, which ached in the calves; then his arms. There was freedom and he saw that the drip had also been taken away. There was just an outline where the sticking-plaster had held it in place. He pushed himself up, gazed around as though recovering from an accident, saw two people watching him from the door.

One of them was Denise. The other was a man: medium height; thirty-fivish; with an alert bony face and straight brown hair. Behind his left ear was a plastic hearing-aid. They moved towards Blake with the muffled tread of those in a sickroom.

'Good evening, Mr Blake,' said the man sardonically, stopping at the edge of the bed. 'I hope you're feeling better for your rest.'

'Forced as it was.'

'I trust the boys looked after you properly.'

'Your goons didn't beat me up.'

'And they were respectful?'

'As much as warders ever are.'

'We couldn't have you wandering around Cape Town with the police of two continents out hunting for you.'

'To say nothing of the Press.'

'For the past ten days the papers have been dominated by your exploits. Or should I say *lack* of exploits. With the exception of those in this household, no-one has any clear idea where you are.'

'Thanks for watching over me.'
The man smiled.
'I've been watching over you for a long time now. Longer than you know.'
'Keep it up.'
'Believe me, I would like to. But your stay with us is coming to an end.'
'You're letting me go free?'
'I wouldn't exactly say that. We'll certainly let you go. But free? I don't think you'll ever be that.'
'You're talking in riddles.'
'Sorry to be so sphinx-like. I assure you all will be revealed soon.'
'And my wife and children. Where are they?'
'We thought you were never going to ask.'
'I would have done earlier, but—'
'Excuses aren't necessary,' he interrupted. 'Most men in your situation would put self before loved ones.'
'You still haven't answered me!' shouted Blake.
'They are safe, well and living on the floor below.'
'When will I see them?'
'Tomorrow morning will be soon enough. Some solid food, a sound night's sleep, and you'll be fit to attend the conference.'
'What conference?'
'The family one.'
He turned to leave and Blake said quickly:
'You still haven't told me who you are.'
The man stopped with his back to him.
'Kretzmer. Mark Kretzmer. You may have heard of me from your wife.'
He walked on and Denise made to follow him. Before leaving she bent over Blake as if to straighten the sheets.
'I warned you,' she whispered. 'That night when you joined the club.'
'Warned me? About what?'
She brushed a lock of hair from his forehead.
'That you *owed* me, and that I'd have to be *paid*.'

CHAPTER FIFTY-TWO

By the morning Blake felt and looked different again. He had removed his beard, clipped most of the grey from his hair, regained the use of his legs. His clothes had also been spruced-up and serviced. The neutral lightweight suit still had the cleaner's label on it, was hanging in a cellophane bag on the pink, veneered wardrobe. Dressed and massaged and lotioned, he felt he could pass for a young-middle-aged man; someone in business; someone with money in the bank and a future not yet behind him.

Breakfast fortified that belief. It was brought to him on a tray by Cleftchin, his mouth chomping. He placed the tray on the dressing-table, pointed to the half-bottle of Oude Meester next to the coffee-pot.

'We thought you'd like a bracer,' he said matter-of-factly. 'Steadies the nerves.'

'We?'

'My partner and I.'

Blake poured some coffee, laced it half-and-half with brandy.

'Where is Boris Karloff?'

'In Cape Town collecting your car.'

'My—'

'The Mercedes you reserved.'

'How did you know about it?'

'We found the bill in your pocket. It should be paid for by now. If your cheque didn't bounce.'

'No fear of that.'

'Not with *your* booty!'

Cleftchin left and it took Blake thirty minutes to kill the bottle. He laid it respectfully on its side, and walked out into the corridor. After the pampered luxury of the bedroom he expected something ostentatious and exotic. But the bare whitewashed walls and quarry-tiled floor could not have been more spartan. He turned a corner and descended to the identical second floor. As he went lower he could see the ocean and the jumbled sprawl of a small port or fishing harbour. The final flight was a spiral staircase made up of broad wooden slats. He walked nervously down, as though he might slip and rupture himself. The living-room came into sight, as white and glaring as the upstairs walls. The fireplace was a hungry black mouth, beyond which a family group had gathered.

He spotted Alastair and Ian first of all, squatting beneath a fishing-net with green bubble-floats. They were reading a comic while Karen looked on, a mixture of pride, possession and anxiety in her face. Standing beside her was the man called Kretzmer. His hand was touching her elbow and Blake thought how *right* they looked together. What a fine and well-suited *couple* they were.

He stopped and tried to turn noiselessly round. His shoes slid on one of the rungs and he caught onto the handrail, hung there like a gymnast. Ian was the first to see him, followed quickly by Alastair. They dropped their comic and darted forward. He tugged himself upright, watched Karen trap the boys in her arms.

'Lo, daddy,' said Ian.

'Hi, dad,' cried Alastair.

'Hello sons,' he answered, his eyes locked with Karen's.

She had on a frothy, white lace dress which ended midway down her thighs. Below it her legs were long, brown, muscular, those of a tennis player. She shooed the boys back to the fireplace, reopened their comic for them, told them to stay there and be good. Blake moved down into the room, waited for her to come to him. She didn't, and crossed over to Kretzmer; halted beside him; took his hand in hers.

'I believe you and Mark have already met,' she said quietly.

'He looked in to wish me ill.'

'You remember me telling you about him. When we first met?'

'Nice to see you've made it up again.'

'We didn't. You did it for us.'

'*Me!* All I did was—'

'Cheat, steal and lie!'

She swung her head away as if he'd hit her, laid it on Kretzmer's shoulder. Blake listened insensibly to her sobbing. He was about to tell her to stow it when another noise gripped his nerve-ends. A tap-tap-tap as though a grub was burrowing its way into the room. He knew who it was without looking. Subconsciously he'd known since he'd first awakened in the house. This time when the boys dashed forward no-one tried to prevent them. They catapulted into Petersen's embrace, knocked the monkey to the floor.

'Grandpa!' they shouted in unison. 'Where have you *been*?'

CHAPTER FIFTY-THREE

It was Alastair who spoke first. In the breathless, wondrous, isn't-life-*fun*?, voice that sometimes made Blake frightened for him.

'Grandad's taking us to Kruger National Park,' he announced. 'To see the lions. And Kimberley to see the Big Hole and watch the men digging for diamonds in the streets.'

'We're going in an aer'plane,' added Ian. 'A red one with wings *this* big!'

He put his arms out and ran excitedly about the room – wheeling, soaring, banking, climbing.

'That's *one* thing about their grandfather,' asserted Karen. 'He not only makes promises – he keeps them!'

'Can we *stay* here with grandad?' asked Alastair.

'For *ever*!' cried Ian, buzzing past him and crash-landing on a sheepskin rug.

'You too, dad,' said Alastair anxiously. 'It's much more better than the bungalow.'

'I'm afraid that's not possible, boys,' replied Petersen for him. 'Daddy has to go away.'

'*Another* business trip?'

'A long one.'

'How long?'

'That depends.'

'A week?' pestered Ian.

'About that,' Blake said.

Ian grinned, scrambled to his feet, became an aeroplane

again – pursued by Alastair, machine-guns blazing as he swooped down on him. Their chase took them from the room, out onto a patio with an azure swimming-pool glinting beyond. With a brief nod in Blake's direction, Karen followed them. Blake turned and watched Petersen retrieve the monkey. The millionaire slipped it into his pocket and then regarded his son-in-law, his button-eyes gleaming.

'Well, Philip. You can count yourself a very lucky man.'

'I can?'

'While I've sheltered you in my house – in my late wife's bedroom – the police have chased themselves stupid. Detective-Inspector Dewhurst ran around this place like a decapitated chicken.'

'Dewhurst was *here*?'

'His questions upset and distressed us all. You were not the only person to need sedation. My daughter did too.'

'Is he *still* in Cape Town?'

'Annoyed and frustrated, he flew back to London yesterday. Hence your release from—'

'Protective custody.'

'I believe that is the euphemism. Since the search here proved fruitless, your presence has been reported in Brazil, Mozambique, Jamaica and Hong Kong. Inspector Dewhurst will be touring the world for the next few months. Who knows, he may meet up with you in – by the way, exactly where *are* you going?'

'I have a choice?'

'It might seem that way to you at first. You will certainly have money.'

'The two million? You don't want it back?'

He and Kretzmer linked glances.

'And have my daughter feel sorry for you again! Penniless and a martyr you might still appeal to her. Rich and hunted and she doesn't want to know.'

'Which leaves the way open for *him*!'

'That is something they must work out for themselves. Without interference from us.'

'He gets my wife. I get your money.'

'Too much money, in fact. What can you possibly spend it on except flight, and still more flight? Start splashing it around and you'll soon be wearing handcuffs. Or is that the latest trend in the underworld? The in-thing in costume jewellery?'

He shook his wrist so that the thick gold bracelet there clattered against his watch.

'I'll give you till Christmas,' he went on evenly. 'Two months. By then you'll be a freak, a cripple. Your head will be turned round backwards from looking behind you. And when you *are* looking over your shoulder, that's when they'll grab you from the front. Two million pounds! You'll be begging every panhandler in the republic to take it from you! From this day on the *world* is your prison. The two million pounds you stole is your sentence. And the warder will be yourself!'

He stopped talking, snapped his fingers in the air.

'Miss Van Heerden,' he ordered. 'Come!'

She entered from the patio. The starch in her uniform crackled as she moved. Her face was a mask to go on a wall. White, frozen, empty.

'The keys, Miss Van Heerden. Give the man his keys.'

She put her hand out to Blake. He felt something cold and steely branding his palm. An ignition key attached to a brace of imitation diamonds. Petersen was not without humour.

'For the Mercedes,' she said dismissively. 'The pleasure is all mine.'

And that was it. They suddenly became preoccupied, talked intimately amongst themselves, behaved as if Blake was no longer there. He closed his fingers over the key and headed blind-eyed to the door.

'Say goodbye to Karen as you leave,' called out Petersen as an afterthought. 'And good luck, Philip. I won't wish you bad. You'll have plenty of that before you're through.'

She was waiting by the car in the tree-fringed, serpentine drive. With her health reviving – the drawn, hunted look retreating from her face – she reminded him of the girl he'd met at a party, all those years ago. A girl he'd betrayed and lost since then. He stood before her, waited for her to speak.

'I'm sorry, Phil,' she murmured. 'About it ending like this.'

'Is it ending?'

'It's over. Didn't Daddy tell you?'

'He was orientally obscure about most things. How Miss Van Heerden took the place of the home-help. How you and the boys came to be here. The mechanics of the coup.'

She placed her fingertips on the windscreen, stroked it as she might do a cat.

'I warned you not to underrate him. His agents began investigating you the moment you left his office. They started in Johannesburg with the crew of the jet. They learnt that one of the stewardesses had been dismissed. When they went to her apartment they found she'd been forced to leave there too. And when they finally caught up with her she had a lot to say about you. *All* of it vindictive.'

'After which your father sent the heavy mob to snatch you from the bungalow.'

She pulled her fingers away as if the cat had proved unfriendly and scratched.

'*I* phoned *him* when I saw your picture on the front page of every rag and scandal-sheet. *Then* he had me collected. But he needn't have bothered. I would've crawled here if I'd had to. With the boys on my back.'

'Thanks for your loyalty.'

'I was tutored by an expert.'

He looked past her to the pool – where the boys were sitting near the edge, throwing pebbles at a rubber sea-horse, red with yellow spots.

'And Alastair and Ian. How will you explain things to them?'

'They're used to being semi-orphans. They only miss you when you're here.'

She stood back from the powder-blue Mercedes and he stooped to open the door. He waited until he was seated, had started the engine before speaking again. He squeezed the wheel with hands that had grown monstrous.

'Later on, Kar, if I sent for you. Would you come?'

'A year ago, if Philip Blake had asked me, I'd have said yes.'

'And now?'

'I couldn't go to Howard Martin. I don't like him.'

'No chance?'

She barely moved her lips.

'No chance.'

The reaction didn't come at once. Not until she, the driveway, and the walled house were hidden by the dust the car threw up. He took a dirt road which, after a violent switchback ride, came out a sign reading: Kalk Bay ½ mile. Cape Town 17. He branched left towards the city and was startled to find his hands wet on the steering-wheel. Salt streaked his features like badly-applied greasepaint, spilled onto the smooth mahogany dashboard.

He shook convulsively in silent pain.

PHASE OUT

CHAPTER FIFTY-FOUR

He took it easy on the long northerly drive to Rhodesia. With Petersen's assurance that he would not denounce him, he spent a week on the journey – stopping overnight at motels on the main tourist routes. To his content the motels had swimming pools (smaller and less blue than the one glimpsed at Falk Bay), and he relaxed in the evenings by floating on the warm, lighted water. He spoke to no-one unless he had to, found all the company he wanted in the flask of brandy carried in his suit. He drank steadily but not excessively, so that he was never exactly tight, never entirely sober.

He was reserved but polite with waiters and garage-hands, cultivated the impression of someone who wasn't looking for trouble. But who would know how to handle himself if trouble should arise. It was the alcohol and not the money that gave him the sense of withdrawal. He could scarcely appreciate that he was so newly and vulgarly rich. Travelling in a car too powerful and spacious for him; with an identity so fictitious that he might as well not exist. There were other issues which he mentally sidetracked, and it wasn't until he reached the Rhodesian border that someone else put the question he most wanted to avoid.

He drove up to the border post at Beit Bridge at three on a hot, steaming, airless afternoon. The car was like a mobile oven; he could have grilled a steak on the bonnet, roasted an animal on the roof. There were two guards on duty and one of them – a lean, slant-shouldered man with eyes the colour of bleached jeans – lounged over to him. The guard put his head to the window and conducted the 'arrival-and-departure routine'. His voice was sleepy, lethargic – it only woke up when he asked:

'What is your purpose in visiting Rhodesia, Mr Martin? Business or pleasure?'

In the quarter-minute that followed Blake was too non-plussed to reply. Business? Pleasure? He was there for neither reason. He was there because, like Everest, Rhodesia existed. Because it made no difference where he went to or why.

The creases on the guard's face deepened. He repeated the question louder, more insistently.

Blake looked up at him and smiled.

'Pleasure,' he lied.

The guard's expression unwound. Blake was no longer suspect, an undesirable crank. Just a little deaf maybe, or slow.

'Have a pleasant stay, Mr Martin. Enjoy yourself.'

'Thanks. I'll certainly try.'

The guard saluted, waved the visitor on.

Blake put his foot hard down on the accelerator and started running.

CHAPTER FIFTY-FOUR

He took it easy on the long northerly drive to Rhodesia. With Petersen's assurance that he would not denounce him, he spent a week on the journey – stopping overnight at motels on the main tourist routes. To his content the motels had swimming pools (smaller and less blue than the one glimpsed at Falk Bay), and he relaxed in the evenings by floating on the warm, lighted water. He spoke to no-one unless he had to, found all the company he wanted in the flask of brandy carried in his suit. He drank steadily but not excessively, so that he was never exactly tight, never entirely sober.

He was reserved but polite with waiters and garage-hands, cultivated the impression of someone who wasn't looking for trouble. But who would know how to handle himself if trouble should arise. It was the alcohol and not the money that gave him the sense of withdrawal. He could scarcely appreciate that he was so newly and vulgarly rich. Travelling in a car too powerful and spacious for him; with an identity so fictitious that he might as well not exist. There were other issues which he mentally sidetracked, and it wasn't until he reached the Rhodesian border that someone else put the question he most wanted to avoid.

He drove up to the border post at Beit Bridge at three on a hot, steaming, airless afternoon. The car was like a mobile oven; he could have grilled a steak on the bonnet, roasted an animal on the roof. There were two guards on duty and one of them – a lean, slant-shouldered man with eyes the colour of bleached jeans – lounged over to him. The guard put his head to the window and conducted the 'arrival-and-departure routine'. His voice was sleepy, lethargic – it only woke up when he asked:

'What is your purpose in visiting Rhodesia, Mr Martin? Business or pleasure?'

In the quarter-minute that followed Blake was too non-plussed to reply. Business? Pleasure? He was there for neither reason. He was there because, like Everest, Rhodesia existed. Because it made no difference where he went to or why.

The creases on the guard's face deepened. He repeated the question louder, more insistently.

Blake looked up at him and smiled.

'Pleasure,' he lied.

The guard's expression unwound. Blake was no longer suspect, an undesirable crank. Just a little deaf maybe, or slow.

'Have a pleasant stay, Mr Martin. Enjoy yourself.'

'Thanks. I'll certainly try.'

The guard saluted, waved the visitor on.

Blake put his foot hard down on the accelerator and started running.